MY LUCKY NIGHT

ROMANCE CAN HAPPEN WHEN YOU LEAST
EXPECT IT...

OLIVIA SPRING

HARTLEY PUBLISHING

To my amazing mum

CHAPTER ONE

Queues.

If there was one thing I hated more than queuing, it was queuing at Christmas.

The lines were always so long. At the supermarket tills as everyone stocked up with enough food to feed ten armies and in the shops where people rushed out to buy things at the last minute.

I glanced at my watch. So far we'd been queuing for an hour. If I was by myself, I'd have left ages ago. But today was different.

I was waiting outside a grotto in Green Park with my five-year-old godson, Paul. Even though I wasn't a fan of Christmas, I'd promised I'd take him to see Santa this year and I couldn't let him down.

Ordinarily, keeping Paul entertained for sixty minutes in the cold would be a challenge. But thankfully his mum, my cousin Bella, had joined us. That meant we'd had a good chat whilst Paul sat on the bench nearby and amused himself playing on her phone.

A little girl came out of the grotto smiling and the boy in front of us was summoned inside. *Hallelujah! That must mean we're next.*

'Come on, Paul,' I called out. 'It's almost time to see Father Christmas.'

'Yippee!' He jumped off the bench so quickly you'd think it was on fire.

'Someone's excited!'

'I am, Aunty Cassie. I've been dreaming about this my whole life.'

So dramatic, bless him.

'I'm just popping to the shops across the road. I'll be back soon to pick you up. Okay, sweetheart?' Bella bent down and kissed Paul gently on the head.

'Okay, Mummy.' He nodded.

'Have fun!' Bella waved.

It wasn't much longer before one of the elves, a woman dressed in a red-and-white striped jumper and green trousers, ushered us into a walkway with warm yellow lighting.

The grotto looked pretty cool. There were sparkly lights, a fireplace with red-and-green stockings hanging from the shelf and a huge Christmas tree, complete with baubles, tinsel and dozens of colourful presents underneath. And of course, sat right beside it was the big man himself.

'Ho, ho, ho!' said Father Christmas. 'So who do we have here, then?'

He looked quite authentic. Over the years I'd seen many versions of Santa Claus, rocking ridiculous fake beards and poorly made red suits, but this guy took the whole Father Christmas gig seriously. I could tell it was his beard and even his stomach looked real. Not like he'd just stuffed a couple of cushions under his jacket.

'This is Paul.' I couldn't resist ruffling his cute dark curly hair.

'Ho, ho, ho! Hello, Paul!' Santa gushed. 'So have you been a good boy this year?'

'Yes, Santa!' Paul jumped up and down before sitting on one of the chairs beside him. He really was such a happy child.

'That's good. So what would you like for Christmas?'

'I would really love a dinosaur Lego kit, *please*,' Paul replied politely.

'Very good choice, young Paul.'

'And a dancing milkshake. Like the one at Aunty's house.'

'Okay, young man!' Santa raised his eyebrow. 'Something tells me you'll be very happy on Christmas Day.'

'Thank you so much, Santa!' Paul grinned.

At least I knew he'd definitely get *one* thing on his list. I reached in my pocket and felt the old dancing milkshake toy, which I'd found when I was clearing out some old boxes.

Note to self to remember to give it to Bella later and double-check she had the dinosaur set. With Santa practically guaranteeing Paul was getting everything he'd asked for, I didn't want him to be disappointed.

'And you?' Father Christmas turned to me.

'Oh no!' I shook my head. 'I'm just here for Paul.'

'Don't you believe in Christmas?'

'Of course!' I said quickly. I absolutely did *not*. I

thought it was all a load of commercialised nonsense, but I couldn't say that, could I?

'Well, then!' He grinned. Come and sit down.'

Paul's eyes widened, willing me to join in on the fun.

Oh, what the hell.

I loosened my green scarf, smoothed down the back of my red coat, then sat on the chair reluctantly.

'Have you been good this year?'

'I have!' That at least was true. I'd been working so hard I hadn't had time to get up to anything bad. I'd had more than my fair share of Quality Street and Celebrations, in fact every chocolate I could find within a hundred-metre radius at the office yesterday, but hopefully that didn't count.

'Excellent! So what would *you* like for Christmas, Cassie?'

I didn't remember telling him my name. They'd written it down when I'd paid for our tickets earlier, though, so maybe he'd looked at the list.

'Oh, I'm okay, thanks.' I smiled. 'Think I've grown out of toys.'

Except the adult kind, of course...

I covered my mouth with my hand to stifle a giggle. I'd treated myself to something at the adult shop last weekend, which I planned to put to good use over the holidays. I'd been single for so long that if I wanted any action, I had to rely on electronic devices.

'It doesn't have to be a toy, Cassie, dear. It can be anything!'

'I don't know.' I shrugged my shoulders.

'Yes, you do!' shouted Paul excitedly.

'Do I?' I scanned my brain for ideas. A new handbag

would be nice. Mine had got a bit tatty around the edges, but the one I had my eye on was super expensive. I'd wait for the January sales to see if it got reduced.

I'd love the Icon hair straighteners everyone raved about too. I reckoned they'd be brilliant at smoothing out my thick curly chestnut hair, but they cost a fortune, so I didn't have the funds for one of those right now. Apart from that, there wasn't anything else I could think of.

'Yes!' Paul seemed convinced. 'Santa, Aunty Cassie wants a boyfriend.'

'Paul!' I shouted, my cheeks burning. 'I do *not*!'

'Yes, you do! You said so when you were talking to my mummy. You said you'd like a nice man to play with!'

Oh God.

Ground, please swallow me up now.

This was *exactly* why you shouldn't have an adult conversation in front of children. When you think they're engrossed in playing games or watching *PAW Patrol* on your cousin's phone, they're really listening to every word you say. How embarrassing.

'Well… I…' I stuttered, trying to think of what to say. This was nuts. As a PA I spoke to managers, CEOs and directors at my firm and managed to act confident most of the time. And yet a five-year-old had somehow got me stumbling over my words.

'Were you telling lies, Aunty Cassie?' Paul folded his arms. 'Mummy says it's *very* naughty to tell lies. And you just said to Santa that you've been nice!' he huffed.

God, this kid was smart.

'Well I *did* say that I would like to try and find a decent man *one day*, but not—'

'So a boyfriend is what you wish for Christmas, young Cassie?'

Couldn't remember the last time anyone had called me *young*, but hey, at thirty-five I had to take the compliments where I could find them.

A boyfriend for Christmas? *Pff.* Of all the things I could wish for, it wouldn't be that. The reason Bella and I had got onto that subject was because she was gushing about the night of passion she'd had with her husband, Mike, when Paul was staying at a friend's house. Bella had asked me if I wanted to get back in the *game* and all I'd said was that yes, I'd like to *play* again *at some point*, but I hadn't meant *now*. I'd only just recovered from my last relationship. I didn't need any more drama or heartache in my life.

Although I didn't mind making Christmas enjoyable for Paul, my plan for the festive break was simple: to stay at home, *alone*. No men, no complications.

There would be no Mum and Dad quizzing me on why I was still single and asking when I was going to settle down. No tree, no turkey or mince pies. It would just be a chill day where I could lose myself in my adult colouring books, watch films or do whatever I wanted. If I felt like it, I might even eat pizza.

Yep. Once I'd wished everyone a merry Christmas and all that jazz, I planned to spend the rest of the day pretending that the whole thing didn't exist. It would be perfect.

I could feel Santa glaring at me. I snapped out of my thoughts. Paul's eyes shone with excitement. Even though a man was a hundred percent *not* what I wanted, it would be easier all around if I just played along.

'Yes!' I feigned enthusiasm. 'I would *love* a boyfriend for Christmas!'

I turned away quickly and rolled my eyes. This was silly. It wasn't like it was going to happen at three o'clock on the day before Christmas Eve, but I'd keep up the act for Paul's sake. The world was hard enough, as he would find out when he was older. It was important to give him something nice to believe in whilst he was young.

Paul had so many disappointments in life to come. Discovering Father Christmas wasn't real, for starters, and learning that the tooth fairy was fake too. I was still scarred by the night I'd woken up and heard my parents arguing about whose turn it was to put the money under my pillow after I lost my tooth. Such a cruel world.

'Well, today is your lucky day! Leave it with me, Cassie. I'm sure I can arrange a very special gentleman for you.' Santa winked.

'Okay, Santa.' I snorted. I didn't mean to, but it was so ridiculous. If there was one word that summed up my life, it definitely wasn't *lucky*. Especially at this time of year.

We posed for the professional photo, Santa gave Paul a little gift and then the elf woman signalled that our time was up.

'Time to go, Paul.' I jumped off the chair. 'Say thank you.'

'Thank you, Santa! I can't wait to play with my dinosaurs on Christmas Day, and Aunty Cassie can't wait to play with her boyfriend!'

I snorted again.

Said so innocently, but little did Paul know there was more chance of it snowing in London on Christmas Day or me finding Santa sitting on my sofa munching gingerbread cookies than there was of that happening. Just as well, really, after what had happened last Christmas. A shooting pain raced straight to my heart.

No. Hopefully next year I'd be ready to dip my toe back in the dating waters again, but not just yet.

CHAPTER TWO

As Paul skipped out of the grotto, a boy walked past clutching a donut. The sugary scent flooded my nostrils and my stomach rumbled.

'Fancy a donut, little one?'

'Yes, please, Aunty!' He beamed.

I took Paul's hand and we headed towards the stand. There was another queue, but Bella was still at the shops, so we had time. If we got some snacks first, it'd make the wait for our photo with Santa more bearable.

Ten minutes later, there were still four people in front of us. I strummed my fingers on my handbag, wondering why it took so long to dish out a few donuts. Just as another person was about to be served, a tall guy strolled straight up to the counter. The woman smiled, put several donuts into a bag, then filled two coffee cups.

What the hell?

So we had to stand here, waiting, whilst he got served straight away?

'Oi! Excuse me!' I shouted. 'There's a queue. You have to wait like the rest of us.'

The guy turned around, stared me straight in the eyes and scowled.

Whoa.

It was like I'd been tasered. His dark eyes burned straight through me.

It wasn't just his eyes that were on fire, it was his whole body. He was hot. Even though he was wearing a thick jacket, scarf and dark jeans, something told me there was a great body underneath those layers.

He narrowed his eyes, scowled again, then turned away. If looks could kill, I'd be dead by now.

If anyone should be angry, it should be us. Nobody liked queues, but they were part of society's rules. Just because he was sexy, it didn't mean he didn't have to follow them.

As he picked the donuts up off the counter, I noticed how thick and shiny his dark hair was. He was probably one of those guys who spent hours in front of the mirror, preening himself like a peacock. I was all for guys looking presentable, but I could never imagine being with a man who took longer to get ready than me.

Despite the chill in the winter air, the lady behind the counter looked like she was overheating. She giggled and blushed like a teenager. When he turned to leave, he flashed her a smile and of course he had the most perfect teeth. All white, even and surrounded by juicy lips.

He'd obviously flirted with her to get served faster. *Shameless.* As he got closer, I shot him a look so dirty he'd have to shower for days to wash it off.

Take that, Mr Queue-Jumper.

Rather than returning the daggers I'd shot, he just smirked and continued walking.

Arrogant prick.

'Still here?'

I turned around and saw Bella clutching two large shopping bags.

'Mummy!' Paul threw his arms around her.

'Yep. We would have got served sooner, but some idiot jumped the queue.'

'That's annoying. At least you've only got three people in front of you now, so it won't be long. How was Father Christmas, sweetie?' Bella planted a kiss on Paul's forehead.

When Paul happily told his mum what Santa had lined up for our Christmas gifts, including a man for me, Bella just smiled like it was the most normal thing in the world. I mean, *come on*.

'You never know, Cass. If you manifest it and put it out into the universe, it can happen.'

'*Yeah, right*,' I scoffed.

If it was that easy, I might as well wish for a million pounds to be deposited into my bank account. A trip to the Caribbean would be nice at this time of year, and what the hell—I should tell the universe that I'd love a penthouse overlooking Green Park too.

Although I loved the idea of positive thinking, I preferred being a realist. And the reality was, this Christmas I would *not* wake up to find some topless hunk standing by the Christmas tree dressed in a Santa hat and nothing else.

Nothing good ever happened at Christmas. Not to me

anyway. I'd accepted that now, though. It was fine. No biggie.

After we got our donuts, I returned to the grotto to collect our photo whilst Bella took Paul to the toilet. We agreed to meet at the exit, so I started making my way there. It had suddenly become congested as if everyone had decided to leave or enter the park at the same time. Just as I scanned my surroundings to see if there was another way out, I felt something solid bash against my head, then a sharp pain in my foot.

There was a man's broad chest in front of me and a large boot resting on mine.

'Ouch!' I yelped. 'Look where you're going!'

'*Pardon. Excusez-moi.*' He quickly removed his foot. *Ooh-la-la.*

Pretty sure I detected a French accent. I came to my senses and looked up and... *oh*.

'It's *you*! The queue-jumper. Typical,' I snapped. 'First you think you're too good to queue and now you're so important that you couldn't possibly put your phone down for two seconds to look where you're going.'

'I have said I am sorry, what do you want that I do? Buy you flowers?' He waved his hands in the air angrily.

I glared at him, for once lost for words. His accent had floored me. It was annoyingly sexy.

And it wasn't just his accent that made my body tingle: it was his face too. He was even hotter up close. He had a hint of stubble, which somehow seemed to accentuate his chiselled jaw and those eyes. They were so deep and hypnotic. If I Googled *tall, dark and handsome*, I wouldn't be surprised to see a photo of him staring back at me.

The sound of a young child shrieking brought me back

to my senses. His arms were folded and his perfect thick brows furrowed, waiting for my response.

'Yes, I mean, no... of course not!' I stuttered. 'Just don't be such a phone robot.'

'Robot?' His frown deepened.

Whenever I walked around London I was guaranteed to bump into at least one phone zombie. You know, people like him who were so glued to their screens that they didn't look where they're going.

'Pay more attention when you're walking and don't jump queues!' I stormed off. I didn't know why, but he'd got under my skin.

I spotted Bella and Paul standing a few metres away.

'Who was *that*?' She smirked.

'That was that dic—' I paused, remembering Paul was there, so I had to mind my language. 'That was the rude guy who jumped the queue.'

'He is *hot*!' Bella's eyes widened.

'Is it because he's wearing too many clothes, Mummy?' Paul's face crumpled. 'Maybe you should tell him to take off his scarf.'

Bella and I looked at each other and chuckled.

'I'm sure Aunty Cassie thinks he should take off a lot more than that...,' Bella whispered.

'Stop it!' I stifled a laugh.

I couldn't deny that the queue-jumping, foot-stomping guy was hot. But his personality was awful.

I'd dated enough over the years to know his type. The good-looking ones were often the worst. Reminded me of Darius. He never felt like he had to make the effort to be a decent human being because women were always falling at his feet. *Ugh.*

My phone rang. I fished it out of my bag.

Oh God.

It was Spencer. My boss. I'd known it was only a matter of time before he called. I contemplated leaving the phone to ring, but knew he'd just keep trying until I picked up.

'Hello,' I said.

'Hi. Where did you put the presents? I can't find them.'

I sighed. I knew he hadn't been listening when I'd told him yesterday. After ordering what felt like hundreds of fancy gifts over the past month for his parents, three children, wife and mistress (I'd had to stop myself several times from screaming about the immorality of him asking me to do that), I'd sat there for hours wrapping them. A sheet of the wrapping paper cost more than I made in an hour, but that was Spencer all over. No expense spared. Shame he didn't feel the same when it came to paying me a decent salary.

'I locked them away in the stationery cupboard. There were too many to fit them anywhere else.'

'And where is the stationery cupboard?'

Jesus. He led such a sheltered life. He came from money. His father had built the real estate company we worked at from scratch, and when he'd retired, Spencer had taken over the reins. In my opinion he had zero talent. It was everyone else in the company that did the work and made him look good.

I'd been his PA for five years and was currently questioning my career choice. In truth, it wasn't my career that was the problem. I enjoyed the organisational aspects of the job and making sure everything ran smoothly. I loved the variety and pace too. It was my boss that was the issue. I knew it was my job to support him and make his life easier, but he literally couldn't do anything by himself. I was surprised that he didn't ask me to wipe his bottom when he went to the loo.

'It's the cupboard in the corridor. Next to the toilets.'

The one you must pass at least five times a day with a sign that has 'Stationery Cupboard' written on the front.

'Oh, yes. Right. And the key?'

I sighed again. 'It's on your desk.' *Right in front of you.*

'Ah, that's what that's for! *Good girl.* Okay, bye.'

So patronising. And not even a thank-you.

'Let me guess…,' said Bella. 'Spencer?'

'Yep. The one and only.'

'But you're supposed to be on holiday for a week.'

'Tell me about it. Thankfully it was only a quick call, so it's fine.'

'If you say so. Be careful, though. Don't let him keep taking advantage of you. Anyway, we're going to head off now. Let me know if you change your mind about coming to ours for Christmas. I hate the idea of you spending it alone.'

'Thanks, but honestly, I'll be fine.'

After giving Bella and Paul a hug, I waved them off and headed towards the tube station. They were getting the bus back to North London so that Paul could see the sights and the Christmas lights.

I loved the way that kids viewed everything with so much enthusiasm. To most adults, an hour on a packed, stuffy bus at this time of year wouldn't be their idea of fun. But to Paul, it was an exciting adventure.

He probably got a lot of his optimism from Bella. She

was always upbeat and positive about everything. Including Christmas and the ability for a man dressed in a red suit with white hair and a beard to make the impossible happen.

Even when she'd got on the bus, she'd opened the window and shouted out, 'Trust the universe!' She really was a believer. Bella had been unlucky in love for a decade until she was reunited with Mike, her first true love, and she was convinced that it was the universe that had brought them together. I was happy for her and of course I wanted to find love and settle down too—I mean, didn't most people? But not all of us got to be that fortunate. Right now, I'd rather be alone than risk getting hurt again.

I glanced at the time on the screen before tucking my phone in my pocket. It was almost 5 p.m., so even though it was already dark, the shops would still be open for hours. For a split second I thought about heading to Oxford Street to see if any shops had started their sales early. Then I thought about all the crowds and the queues... not a good idea.

I'd just go home and have a chilled night. Apart from the odd Christmas party in the last couple of weeks, if I wasn't working late, most of my evenings were low-key. I was used to going back to an empty home.

As I walked to Green Park tube station, my phone started ringing again.

Spencer. *Great*.

'Cassie, sweetheart. Bit of a crisis...'

'What's happened?' I rolled my eyes. Last Saturday he'd called me at 7 a.m. with a 'major emergency': he couldn't find the caviar or foie gras I'd ordered for his dinner party that evening.

To most people, an emergency would be breaking a limb, chronic tooth pain or, I don't know, not having enough money to pay the electricity bill. But to Spencer it was making sure he had his precious bloody caviar. Talk about upper-class problems.

I'd reminded him that it had been delivered to his house the night before so was probably sitting somewhere in his kitchen. Why he hadn't checked before calling and waking me up was beyond me.

'I need you to get me one of those fancy hairdryers that everyone's going on about.'

See? It wasn't a crisis after all. I had visions of having to go into the office and clean up some major disaster, but this wasn't a problem. I'd already ordered the Icon hairdryer last month. There was no way I would have got it otherwise. Despite the hefty price tag, I'd known it was going to sell out, so I'd got ahead of the curve.

His wife, Priscilla, had hinted she'd like one (Priscilla often dropped things that she wanted into conversations as she knew I'd make sure it was arranged). Last year it was a Tiffany diamond necklace. Think the year before it was three pairs of those fancy Louboutin red-bottom shoes. *Oh, to have money.*

'It's already sorted,' I replied smugly. 'It's not with the gifts in the stationery cupboard. It was in the pile of presents you took home last week.'

'Yes, I know. And that's the problem…'

'Problem?' I frowned. How could the fact that I'd been organised enough to buy the perfect gift for his wife before it sold out be a problem?

'Yes… you see, Priscilla has a tendency to get excited

about Christmas and sometimes she opens gifts before the big day.'

'Yeah…?' I still didn't follow.

'So Priscilla just called and, well, she opened it…'

'And?' She was an adult, so why was it such a big deal that she knew what her present was in advance? Considering she'd already hinted about having one, it was hardly a secret.

'It's just that, when I met Sally for lunch earlier, she also asked for one. So I'd planned to give *her* the hairdryer and get something else for Priscilla. But now I'm in a bit of a pickle, because Priscilla knows it's been purchased, so if I give it to Sal, all hell will break loose. That's why I need you to get me another one. ASAP.'

What. A. Dick.

Right now, I wanted to take my phone and stamp on it. Not only had my arse of a boss called me repeatedly on my day off, but now he was asking—no, sorry, *demanding*—that I find an item that I knew had been sold out for ages on the day before Christmas Eve, so that he could keep his mistress happy. This was wrong on so many levels that I didn't even know where to start.

As far as I was concerned, infidelity was the worst. It was so hurtful, damaging and unforgiveable. Especially when there were kids involved. Knowing Spencer was having an affair and not being able to speak up about it and tell his wife what a scumbag he was already preyed on my conscience daily, and now this? I didn't get paid enough to deal with this shit.

'Did you hear me, Cassie?' He raised his voice. 'I need that hairdryer by tomorrow morning. In fact, tonight would be better.'

My cheeks burned. There was so much I wanted to say to him, but I needed this job. My boiler had broken down two weeks ago and the new one had cost a fortune. I'd whacked it on my credit card because I didn't have the cash. I needed to pay it off in full by next month—otherwise, I'd get hit with interest.

Deep breath. It's just work. His personal life is not my concern. Deep breath. Deep breath…

'Spencer,' I said firmly. I counted to three to try and calm myself down. 'That hairdryer is sold out. *Everywhere*. I know this because Catherine, Hector's PA, was trying to get hold of one on Monday for his wife and she contacted all the big department stores and top salons and trawled the internet and there was nothing. There's no way I can get hold of one this side of Christmas and definitely not *tonight*.'

'Cassandra…' He paused. 'Is it not your job to make my life easier? Is that not what I pay you for?'

'Yes, but—'

'So if you fail to get this for me, will you be doing your job?'

'It's not that simp—'

'And if my wife and girlfriend don't both get what they want for Christmas, what do you think is going to happen? Do you think my life will become easier?'

'No, but—'

'Divorce is expensive, Cassie. I'll have to make cutbacks to pay for it. That won't be good. For either of us. Getting that hairdryer is *imperative*. Do you understand? Find a way to get it or find a new job.'

He hung up.

Bastard.

So much for a nice chilled evening and enjoying my time off. Now I'd have to spend the whole night searching for this bloody gift.

And after Catherine had spent days trying to track one down without success, I didn't rate my chances.

CHAPTER THREE

I fought my way through the crowds along Oxford Street. Only the mad or desperate braved coming here this close to Christmas. The pavement was packed with people ladened with bags and walking at a snail's pace. Still, I supposed the thousands of shimmering lights that were draped along the street gave it a warm glow.

I walked through the doors of Allman's, the store that was probably my last hope. I'd already been to Selfridges, John Lewis, Fenwick, Boots and everywhere I could think of, but unsurprisingly they were sold out.

Mariah Carey's 'All I Want for Christmas' blared from the speakers as I headed towards the beauty department. I scanned the tools section but couldn't see the dryer, so went to look for someone to help. After searching for several minutes, I caught the attention of a shop assistant.

'Excuse me, do you have an Icon hairdryer please?'

'You're joking, right?' She burst out laughing.

Okay, love, no need to be rude.

'I know it's a big ask, but don't you have one

anywhere? Maybe at the back of the stock cupboard? On display? I'll take anything. My job literally depends on it.'

'Sorry, but everyone knows they sold out weeks ago.' She rolled her eyes. 'We should get some more in January. Yes, madam.' She smiled at the woman behind me. 'How can I help?'

I trudged out of the store. This was so unfair. How was it right that I had to spend the rest of my day off running around London to find a gift just because my bloody boss couldn't keep his dick in his pants? If he was faithful to Priscilla, none of this would be happening. *Men*. This was one of the many reasons I didn't want a boyfriend.

It was important that I kept trying, though. Not just to keep my job, but also for the sake of his wife. And *oh God* —his poor kids. Imagine the arguments if she found out his dirty little secret? Their Christmas Day would be ruined. Although I hated his despicable actions, if I could help those children have a peaceful holiday, I had to do what I could.

As I walked down Bond Street, I scrolled through different websites on my phone praying that I'd find something, then I remembered: Fortnum & Mason. I hadn't tried there yet. It was a fancy store based near Green Park, so really I should've gone there first when Spencer had called. It was a long shot, but worth a try.

Surprise, surprise. Like everywhere else, they were sold out.

I took out my phone and continued searching. Suddenly I felt something solid.

'Look where you walk!' boomed a deep voice.

I looked up from my screen. It was *him*: the hot but very rude guy.

'You walked into me!' I scowled. As I looked down I realised that this time *I* had my foot on *his* black boots and quickly stepped back.

Oops.

'No. Now you are the, how you say, the *phone robot*. You focus too much on your phone that you do not see what is in front of you.'

Touché.

I'd walked straight into that one, pardon the pun. Hearing him quote back what I'd said to him in the park earlier stung. Okay, maybe I wasn't fully alert. I wasn't about to admit that to him, though. It wasn't *all* my fault.

'Well, you were standing in the middle of a busy street, which is a stupid thing to do at Christmas.'

'I do not have time for this,' he huffed and walked off.

Dickhead.

I went back to look at the website I'd stumbled on. I wasn't sure if it was legit, but they claimed to have two products in stock, yes!

How much? That was daylight robbery.

I'd only walked a few yards when I hit something solid. Him. *Again.* This was ridiculous. And now that was twice he'd caught me being a phone zombie. I quickly put my mobile in my pocket before he called me out on being a shameless hypocrite.

'Are you following me?' I snapped.

'This is a public street, *non*?' He rolled his eyes. 'You do not own it.'

'You don't have to be so rude!' My nostrils flared. 'You're French, right?'

'*Oui…*' His eyes narrowed.

'Well, you really aren't helping disprove the stereotype.'

'What stereotype?'

'About some of them not being... well, you know... not being the most polite people in the world.' I tried to be tactful. I was sure the majority of the French population was nicer than him. Bella's friend Sophia had lived in France and loved it. But this guy was single-handedly giving the nation a bad name.

His mouth fell open. Annoyingly, he had a very sexy mouth, but that wasn't the point. He was still a dickhead.

'I am not rude. Just honest. It is *you* who is not very friendly, *Mademoiselle Fraise*.'

'I *am* friendly!' I folded my arms. Why did people always say that? I wasn't rude. Impatient? Sometimes, yes. Hard? A little. I had to protect myself, that was all. I considered myself like a chocolate truffle. Hard on the outside, but with a soft centre. They'd know that if they bothered to take the time to get to know me. 'And what did you just call me?'

'Mademoiselle *Fraise*.'

'What does that even mean?'

'Miss Strawberry.' He smirked. 'You wear a red coat with a green scarf and hat. Like strawberry, *non*?'

'Don't call me that.' I assumed he meant it as an insult, which annoyed me even more. He was so irritating.

I felt my phone vibrating. *Spencer*.

'Hello?' I wanted to say *what the hell do you want now*? but I resisted the temptation.

'So? Have you got it yet?'

Seriously? We only spoke an hour and a half ago. I'd

like to think I was good at my job, but I wasn't a miracle worker.

'No, I haven't. Like I explained earlier, I don't think you understand how popular it is. Every woman I know would love to get their hands on an Icon hairdryer, but it's impossible. I told you. They sold out weeks ago. I've been everywhere.'

'What about online? There must be one *somewhere*.'

'I've tried. I did find one a minute ago…'

'Excellent! I told you it wasn't impossible. All you had to do was look properly—'

'But it was being sold for over a thousand pounds and the website looked dodgy, so…'

'A thousand pounds? For something that just blows out hot air? That's, what, four times the original price! Ridiculous! Find it cheaper somewhere else.'

'But—'

'No buts, Cassie. Just get it done. *Tonight*.' He hung up.

'Arsehole!'

'*Comment?*' The French guy scowled.

'Not you.' I mean, yeah, he probably was an arsehole too, but after he'd just called me rude I wasn't about to insult him to his face and prove him right. 'My stupid boss wants me to get something that's impossible to find, like I'm some sort of magician.'

'Maybe I can help?'

'*You?*' I scoffed. 'Yeah, right!'

'Fine!' He turned on his heels.

Rule number one we'd learnt as children was not to trust strangers. Or maybe it was not to talk to them. Either way, it boiled down to the same thing. In this big bad world, most people were just out for themselves. They rarely did things to help others. Which was why I needed to keep my guard up. Just in case. That way I couldn't get scammed or taken advantage of. Being cautious was always best.

What if he *could* help, though? I'd already tried everything, so I didn't see what he'd be able to do that I hadn't. Then again, I was desperate. I had nothing to lose by asking.

'Wait!' I quickly ran to catch up with him. 'You said you could help? What did you hear when you were listening to my conversation?'

'You are looking for a hairdryer, yes?'

'Not just any hairdryer.' I rolled my eyes. 'The Icon hairdryer. I doubt you've even heard of it.'

'Why not? Because I am a man?'

I admit that was kind of what I was thinking. All the guys I'd dated didn't have a clue about women's products or gadgets. One of my exes thought the diffuser attachment for my hairdryer was some kind of back massager, for goodness' sake. So I'd just assumed he was the same, which was bad on my part.

'Erm… so you've heard of it?'

'*Oui*. I am hairdresser.'

Aha. That explained the lovely hair. If he told me he'd starred in a L'Oréal shampoo advert I'd believe him.

'So do you know how to get one, then? Maybe from a wholesaler or a special secret hairdresser retailer or something?'

'*Oui.*'

'Oh my God!' My eyes widened. 'That would be *amazing*! But the thing is, I need it kind of, like, *now* and

I'm assuming that you're a hairdresser in France, so would you know how to find one here, in London?'

'I would not say I could if I did not.'

A simple yes would have sufficed. Looked like I needed to start calling him Mr *Sarcastic* Queue-Jumper.

'No need to be snappy,' I sneered. 'It's just they're hard to get, so it's understandable that I'd be a bit sceptical. But if you could just tell me where to find one, I would be grateful.'

'How grateful exactly?' He smirked.

'I mean, obviously a *lot*.' I didn't think it was wise to tell him that my boss had said that if I didn't get the hairdryer to him by tomorrow morning, he'd be gifting me my P45 for Christmas.

'I am confident I can get this dryer for you, but I would like you to do something for me,' he said with a glint in his eye.

Was he for real?

'You dirty little pervert! If you think that I'm desperate enough to perform some sort of sexual favours just to get a hairdryer, you can forget it!'

'That is what you think I want?' he laughed. 'Do not flatter yourself, *ma chérie*.'

Oh.

My cheeks burned. I wished the ground would swallow me up.

'So what do you want, then?' I huffed.

'Tell me where is Carnaby Road.'

'What? All you want is directions?'

'Yes. I am lost. That is why I keep stopping.'

So this guy was going to help me track down London's most coveted Christmas gift and all he wanted in return was for me to point a few fingers in the air at some streets? Sounded fishy…

'That makes no sense. You know this is the twenty-first century, right? Why don't you just look on the blue map direction things they have on every street in London, or—*hello?*—use Google Maps like everyone does?'

'I do not have my phone.'

'Who comes out without their phone?' I scoffed.

'Somebody who has just walked into a rude woman in the park who tells him to not be a—how you say? *Phone robot*—so decides to leave it at the hotel and explore the city the old-fashioned way.'

I opened my mouth to speak, then quickly closed it again.

'Oh…' was all I managed once I regained the power of speech.

So he'd listened to my comment and taken it to heart. I felt a flash of guilt. Obviously I hadn't meant for him not to use his phone at all. Just to watch where he was going…

'Okay, but you could just ask someone else and then you wouldn't have to help me.'

Shit. I shouldn't have said that bit. After all, I needed his help, so it was stupid of me to give him a reason not to. I didn't know why, but he just pushed all my buttons.

'Christmas is a time to help people, *non*?'

He was right. Don't get me wrong. As much as I disliked this time of year, I wasn't a Grinch or anything. If a bunch of merry carol singers rang my bell, I wouldn't slam the front door in their faces.

Even though I hated the holidays, it didn't mean I believed no one else should enjoy them or that I didn't like making them nice for other people. It just hadn't been a fun time of year for me and I wouldn't wish the kind of bad luck I'd experienced at Christmas on anyone. That was why every year, as well as doing the usual stuff for family and friends, I tried to do three good deeds.

Before I'd met Bella and Paul earlier, I'd dropped off some flowers at my local hospital and said the nurses could give them to whoever they felt needed cheering up the most.

After that, I'd left some colouring books and new crayons in the paediatric wing. I wanted to hand out some gloves and socks to the homeless, but the queue in the shop I'd gone to buy everything from was so long that I'd had to leave. Otherwise I would have been late meeting Paul and Bella.

Maybe helping this guy could be my third good deed. Giving him directions would take all of five seconds, but it could still count. And of course if he was able to help me, which I still wasn't convinced he could, then I'd get to keep my job too. Seemed like I was the clear winner in this deal, which probably meant it was too good to be true.

'It should be, but usually most people are just out for themselves. Anyway, I'll give you directions.' Whether he could really help me or not, it didn't matter. Even though I thought he was rude, I'd show him that I wasn't.

'Give me your phone,' he hissed.

'What? Why?'

I hesitated. Living in London all my life had made me suspicious. I wondered if this was a scam where I handed it over and then he'd run off.

'Do you always ask so many questions? To make a phone call, of course.'

I unlocked the screen and passed it to him reluctantly.

After typing something into the internet browser, he switched to the call screen, pasted in the number, then hit the dial button.

'I want to speak to Andrew.' *Whoa.* Clearly he'd missed the lesson on polite phone etiquette. 'It is…' He sighed. 'He will know who I am.'

Ugh.

So arrogant. Bet he was one of those annoying people who waltzed straight to the top of a nightclub queue and barked 'don't you know who I am?' to the person in charge of the guest list.

'Okay.' He hung up. Wow, he didn't say goodbye to people either? 'He is not there. I will try later.'

Andrew probably *was* there but either didn't have a clue who this guy was or didn't want to speak to him. Couldn't blame him.

'Now you give me directions.'

'Er, I thought the deal was that you helped me to find the dryer?'

'I told you, he is not there.'

Likely story. I knew he couldn't help. I'd tell him where he needed to go and then continue looking myself.

'Whatever. So I'm assuming you meant that you need to get to Carnaby *Street*?'

'Oui, oui, c'est ça.'

'Okay, so…' I racked my brains trying to think of the best route. 'Um, well, the simplest way, I suppose, is if you walked all the way down to the bottom of Piccadilly, which is the road we're on now, then turn left-ish onto Regent Street and then you kinda walk all the way up… well, not *all* the way, just until you get to… what's the name of that road again?' I asked myself. 'It's near the Apple Store, but not on the same road…'

Oh gosh. I wasn't doing a very good job of explaining.

'Continue,' he commanded.

'Well, that way probably is quite long. I mean, really, it's best to go around the back, y'know, up New Bond Street and then turn right when you get to…' *Dammit.* Why didn't I pay more attention when I was walking?

He raised his eyebrow as if to say: *Are you really from London? Do you even know what you're talking about, woman?*

'It's kind of hard to explain. I'd know the roads if I saw them, I'm just rubbish with actual street names.'

A grin spread across his face. Was he mocking me? *Charming.*

'There's no need to laugh. Remember, I'm just trying to help *you*.'

'I do not laugh at you,' he purred.

I'd been trying really hard not to let his accent affect me, but I was failing miserably. The way he spoke was so lush he could probably read the instruction leaflet for constipation tablets and still make it sound sexy.

'Why are you smiling, then?'

'You say you know the names of the streets if you see them, *oui*?'

'Yeah, easily.'

'So you can *show* me.'

There went that accent again. It was so hypnotic. At this rate he could ask me to rob a bank and I'd say yes.

But then Lady Logic entered my head and reminded me that he was a stranger. A very handsome one, but still a stranger. For all I knew he could be dodgy. He could be part of an organised gang that targeted women, then kidnapped them. You know, like in that film *Taken*. Except my dad wasn't Liam Neeson, so there'd be no one to rescue me.

'Um, why don't I just show you on my phone instead?' *Yes*. Just like I'd suggested earlier. That was more sensible.

'How long it will take to walk there?'

'Shouldn't be more than fifteen minutes. Twenty tops.'

'Well, if you take me, when we arrive, perhaps I can try Andrew again and ask about the dryer.'

Dammit. I'd forgotten about that. Made sense. Although I didn't like this guy and we'd probably spend the whole time arguing, he didn't seem dangerous. We were in public and I'd be leading the way, so hopefully it'd be fine. And let's face it. It'd take me longer to track down the gift by myself. Assuming he was telling the truth about this Andrew guy, of course…

'Yeah, okay.'

'*Bien.*' He nodded. '*Comment tu t'appelles*—what is your name, Strawberry?'

I narrowed my eyes.

'If I tell you my real name, will you stop calling me that?'

'Maybe, but I cannot promise.' He smirked.

'Please try.' I rolled my eyes. 'My name is… *je m'appelle Cassie*,' I said, pleased I'd spoken a whole two words in another language.

'*Tu parles français?*' His eyes widened.

'Ha! No.' The corners of my mouth twitched. 'That's about my limit.' I should've paid more attention in my French lessons at school.

'And *you*, Mr Queue Jumper? What's your real name?'

He wasn't the only one who could dish out annoying nicknames.

'Nicolas.'

'Okay, *Nicolas*.' I walked ahead. 'Come on. Let's get you to Carnaby Street.'

CHAPTER FOUR

We passed the Ritz and Fortnum & Mason again. As much as I hated Christmas, I had to admit, they both had pretty festive displays. Their buildings were covered in sparkling lights, and tourists stopped to take photos of the iconic buildings on their phones.

'So what's on Carnaby Street, then?' I attempted to make conversation as we crossed the road and headed back up towards Dover Street. If we were going to spend almost half an hour together, I'd rather it wasn't awkward. 'I suppose you're going shopping?'

I wondered if he'd left it until the last minute like many of the men I knew. If my brother could go shopping on Christmas morning, he would, and as for my dad, Mum had given up relying on him to get gifts for his family and did it all herself weeks in advance.

Nicolas probably wanted to get something for his girl-friend—or should that be *girlfriends*, plural?—to bring back to France. I knew it was wrong of me to presume, but there was no way this guy was single. I'd seen how he'd flirted with that donut lady earlier and made her melt like hot ice cream.

'No, I want to see the Christmas lights. I hear they are very cool there.'

'You're interested in seeing the Christmas lights? You'll need to see much more than just Carnaby Street, then. Let's take the scenic route.'

'*Parfait!*'

Wait...what was I doing? The deal was to take him straight to Carnaby Street and that was it. But I'd said I'd do it now, so I couldn't take it back.

'One condition, though,' I added quickly.

'Condition?'

I'd forgotten about the language barrier thing. Bella taught English to foreign business professionals, so she'd be much better at communicating. I needed to simplify the way I spoke.

'I'll take you the scenic route and extend our little tour, as long as you're not a dick.'

'*Dick?*' He frowned. 'It is a little soon for you to talk about my penis, *non*?'

'What?' My eyes widened. 'No! I didn't mean...' I winced.

Oh Jesus. Now he thought I wanted to sleep with him, which I absolutely, positively did *not*.

I mean, of course he was sexy. On a scale of one to ten he was easily a fifteen (not technically accurate, I know, but...). I couldn't remember seeing a guy this hot. Maybe on TV or in a celebrity magazine, but not in real life. Nicolas was the kind of guy that fantasies were made of.

But like I'd said earlier, I wasn't looking for romance right now. And even if I was, I'd never go for a guy like him. Firstly, he was from another country. Secondly, he was definitely one of those playboy, date several women at a time types.

I bet he was only into one-night stands too. Despite dating a fair amount over the years, I'd never had one before. I knew myself. I wouldn't be able to hack the whole not getting attached thing and the guy would inevitably break my heart.

Even if I could detach my feelings, nothing would happen with this Nicolas guy. For a start he'd have to actually like me, and I'd put money on the fact that he exclusively dated models or something. Whilst I was five foot seven, so not completely short, and tried to keep fit and healthy, it wasn't like I had a string of hot guys knocking down my door.

Anyway, what was I even saying? Never mind *him* liking *me*. *I* didn't like *him*. He was rude and arrogant. I could never be attracted to someone like that.

Nope. *Never gonna happen*. That vibrator I'd bought for Christmas was a wise investment. Sex toys didn't break up with you or make you feel like you weren't good enough. They gave you pleasure without the pain. And they had impeccable manners. Which was more than I could say for this guy…

'Let me make one thing clear:' I folded my arms, 'I am not interested in your *dick*. I was trying to say that I would extend our little tour slightly if you didn't act like a *dickhead*, which means idiot. But I'm not sure you're capable of that.'

'*Je rigole*, Strawberry!' Nicolas smirked. 'I make a joke. Of *course* I understand the word. But what I do not understand is why you think I am dickhead?' The way he said *dick-head* like it was two separate words, in his deep, thick accent, made me smile. I quickly put my serious face back on.

'Where would you like me to start, *Mr Queue-Jumper*?'

I explained how disgusted I was with how he'd acted at the donut stand, and he just laughed, then shook his head.

'It is not what you think. I wait in the line for almost half an hour. But when I arrive at the front and order coffee and donuts, I realise I did not have my wallet. So I return to the hotel to get money. The woman said I did not have to queue again—just come to the front and take everything. So that is what I did.'

Oh.

That would explain his dirty look when I'd shouted at him. Now I was the one that felt like an idiot.

'Right, erm, fair enough.' I bit my lip. 'I'll take you to Berkeley Square,' I added quickly, attempting to mask my embarrassment. 'So we can walk past Annabel's.'

'So does that mean you do not think I am dickhead…?' The corner of his mouth twitched.

'Haven't decided yet.' I would've mentioned how annoyed I was about him bumping into me and stepping on my foot, but I'd done exactly the same thing as him, so…

'I will show you, *Cassie*, that I am not.'

On second thoughts, maybe he was better off calling me *strawberry* after all, because I liked how he said my name *way* too much:

Cass-seee…

Mmmm… It sounded *so* erotic somehow. Maybe because I wasn't used to hearing a guy say it outside of work. I think the last time a man had screamed my name was when my gingerbread latte was ready in Starbucks.

'Who is Annabel?'

'It's some fancy members' club for the rich and famous, so normal people like us wouldn't be allowed in, but tourists usually stand outside just to see the lights.' I thought about the photos that always popped up on Instagram at this time of year.

'Okay.'

We still had a way to go before we reached Carnaby Street and I'd much rather we were civil, so I decided to make some polite conversation to pass the time.

'So where in France are you from?'

'Paris.'

'Cool.' I probably could have guessed. Something about his vibe said that he was from the city. He looked like he could be one of the hot love interests in a show like *Emily in Paris*. His English was pretty good too. But I wasn't about to tell him that. 'And is this your first time in London?'

'No. I have been here before for work, but this is the first time I come mainly for pleasure.'

Jesus, Mary and Joseph. The way he said *pleasure* sent tingles down my spine. *Focus, Cassie.* He didn't mean *that* kind of pleasure.

Honestly, I didn't know what had come over me.

'So you work in hairdressing? You're definitely a good advert for your job. You have great hair.' As soon as the words flew out of my mouth, I cringed. I needed to learn the difference between making polite conversation and gushing. Fifteen minutes ago I'd hated this guy's guts and now I was lusting over his locks.

'*Merci*, you too.'

'Er, thanks…' I resisted the temptation to say *yeah right* and accepted the compliment. I touched my hair nervously, suddenly feeling self-conscious about my split ends. My hairdresser always told me to get a trim every six weeks, but it'd been at least six months since a pair of scissors had been anywhere near my head. Nicolas was probably analysing my hair right now, thinking about how he could fix it. Thank goodness my hat covered up my roots, which really needed a touch-up too.

'And you? What is your job?'

'I'm a PA—personal assistant.'

'Cool. Very important job. Helping to keep people organised.'

'I try,' I said. 'Here it is.' I stopped on the road opposite Annabel's. Outside was a huge 2D tree, which looked over forty feet high. It was covered in fake snow and dressed with giant gold baubles and lights, and there was an extravagant copper star at the top. Even the doormen outside were dressed in festive red coats.

'Wow. This is *magnifique*. If you did not show this to me, I would never know that it existed. Take a picture for me.'

'*Please*?' I snapped. I knew the polite conversation couldn't last long.

'*Comment?* What?' He frowned.

'Polite people usually say *please* when they're asking for something.'

'*Mon Dieu.*' He closed his eyes, took a deep breath, opened his eyes again, then pasted on a fake grin.

God, I hadn't been wrong earlier when I'd said he had

perfect teeth. Now we were just a few feet apart, they looked even more impressive. *Bastard.*

'*S'il vous plaît, Mademoiselle Strawberry. Pardon, s'il vous plaît, Mademoiselle Cassie*, please: can you be kind and take a photo, *please*? That is better for you?' He cocked his head.

'It'll do, I suppose,' I huffed. I knew I shouldn't feel guilty about the fact that he didn't have his phone with him, but the truth was, I did. But only a little.

It hadn't escaped my attention that if I took pictures, I would have to send them to him, which would mean we'd need to exchange numbers. But that wasn't why I'd agreed. I was just helping him. Doing a good deed. That was it. Nothing more.

I snapped a few photos of him standing in front of the giant tree, then led him over to New Bond Street, which was lit up with lights in the shape of white peacock feathers.

Next we walked over to Regent Street, which had a stunning display of handcrafted illuminated flying angels and spirits, before walking through to Carnaby Street, where the pink neon lights glowed above us.

'So this is it, then…' My voice trailed off. 'Our final destination: Carnaby Street.' Even though Christmas definitely wasn't my favourite time of year, this hadn't been completely awful. The lights looked nice and having to talk to Nicolas hadn't been as painful as I'd thought.

'Thank you for the tour.' Nicolas stood in front of me and I did everything I could to avoid staring directly at him. His dark, sparkly eyes were annoyingly hypnotic. 'Give me your phone. I will try Andrew again.'

'Oh, yeah, course,' I stuttered. He took my mobile,

dialled the number, then started pacing backwards and forwards up the street whilst he spoke.

He returned a minute later.

'Andrew is still not in the salon, but he will return in one hour. I can call then.'

An hour? Dammit. I really needed to know one way or another if he was legit. The shops would be open until around nine o'clock, but it was still cutting it fine.

'Is there no way to reach him on his mobile to check whether he has one or not? Or maybe there's someone who can check in the salon for him?'

'You do not think I try this already?' He rolled his eyes.

'Okay! Don't get your knickers in a twist!' God, he was annoying.

'Knickers?'

'It means no need to get so worked up—snappy.'

'The phone lady try to call him. No answer. And if he have the dryer, he would not just leave it for someone to find. He would hide it.'

Made sense. Someone with light fingers could get a lot of money for selling one of those.

'Fair enough. I better get going, then. Try and see if I can find it somewhere else.'

'Or you can help me with something for one hour until I call again.'

'Help you with *what* exactly?' I raised my eyebrow.

'To find other places.' He reached in his pocket and took out a piece of paper. 'This afternoon I discover a list of ten things to do in London at Christmas and I would like to do them all.'

'Ten?' I gasped. 'You want to visit *ten* places in an hour?

'Not in an hour. I just want to do them all today. I have done some already. I visit the grotto, do Christmas shopping and now I see the lights. So there are only seven more things.' It was already after seven o'clock, so I wondered if we'd have time.

'Let me see.' I held out my hand and he gave me the sheet of paper. I glanced over the list:

Ten Things to Do in London at Christmas

1. See the Christmas lights
2. Visit a Christmas grotto
3. Visit a Christmas market
4. Go Christmas shopping at a famous London store
5. See the London skyline
6. Eat Christmas dinner
7. Go ice-skating
8. Go to a Christmas party
9. Drink mulled wine
10. Enjoy a kiss under the mistletoe

Actually, it didn't seem too challenging. Some things could be ticked off pretty quickly and—*hello*...

My eyes widened as I read point number ten:

Enjoy a kiss under the mistletoe

Oh...

If this was Christmas next year and I had the opportunity to kiss a hot French guy, *maybe* I'd be up for it. But that would *not* be happening tonight. Pretty he might be, but my lips weren't going anywhere near someone like him.

The idea of dragging myself around more shops looking for this dumb dryer filled me with dread, so it would be easier to just wait an hour and see what happened. If this Andrew guy wasn't back in the salon by then, I'd definitely need to leave Nicolas and figure out a Plan B.

He might be a twat, but if I helped him for an hour, I could definitely feel satisfied that I'd done my proper third good deed. Just taking him to Carnaby Street somehow didn't seem like it was enough.

'Okay. Not sure how much we can fit into an hour, but some things are super easy to do. Others, I don't think I'll be able to help with…'

I passed the list back quickly before I started thinking about point number ten. Not because I wanted to do it, of course. I'd be at home relaxing long before that. 'Come on, if we're going to tick things off this list, we'd better get going.'

CHAPTER FIVE

W hilst Nicolas looked for the gents, I checked the beauty department at Liberty's. Again. You know, just in case a hairdryer had magically appeared in the last hour, which was when I'd checked. Of course it hadn't.

My phone pinged. Better not be Spencer chasing me. *Phew.* It was a message from Bella. I opened it to see a selfie of her and Paul on the bus grinning. *So cute.* They were safely back at home now.

Actually, on the subject of keeping safe, although Nicolas didn't seem like an axe murderer (not that I could be sure that I'd ever met one), it wouldn't hurt to drop Bella a quick text to tell her where I was. Just in case. That was what I used to do in the dark ages whenever I went on a date with a guy I'd met online. Not that I was comparing this to a date, of course.

Me

Hey! Just letting you know I'm still in the West End. Showing some French guy (the rude one I met earlier) the

Christmas lights. He might be able to help me find a gift that stupid Spencer needs urgently.

Literally seconds after I sent the Whatsapp message, Bella came online and started typing.

Bella

Oooh! And this 'rude' guy wouldn't happen to be the tall, dark and handsome man from the park by any chance?

Me

Might be.

Bella

So Santa has started working his magic already! He promised you'd have a guy to play with for Christmas and *voilà*, here he is…

I was glad this was a text and not a video call so Bella couldn't see how hard I was rolling my eyes right now.

Me

It was just a coincidence. Nothing to do with bloody Santa!!!

Me

It's Christmas for God's sake. London is filled with tourists, so the chance of bumping into one who needs directions is higher than usual, that's all.

Me

And before your romantic imagination starts going into overdrive, it's completely innocent. I've shown him the lights, taken a few photos and now I'm going to show him a few other places for an hour until he finds out if his contact can help me.

Bella

Yeah, SURE! Completely innocent…

And you mentioned photos? Taken any with him in them?

That was a point. Maybe I should send Bella a pic, just in case she'd forgotten what Nicolas looked like. Just as a precaution. You know, in case I disappeared and the police needed to know who the last person to see me was. I quickly attached the photo and pressed send.

Bella

Oooh, HELLO!! I know I'm a taken woman, but he is even hotter than I remember!!

Bella added a row of love heart eyes emojis.

I admit, she wasn't wrong.

Bella

What's his name?

Me

Nicolas.

Bella

Just like the French Santa Claus…

Bella

I told you! This is the universe at work. It's happening Cass!

Me

Purlease!!

. . .

I loved Bella, but sometimes she really did live in cloud cuckoo land.

Bella

Anyway, why are you wasting time texting me when you could be smooching with the hot Saint Nic? Go! xxx

That was a point—not the smooching bit, *obviously*. I meant I'd better head back to the entrance to meet him.

Me

I told you, it's not like that! I'll message later.

When I got to the doors, I saw Nicolas was outside staring at a festive window display.

I went and tapped him on his arm. It felt so firm. I knew what I'd thought when I'd first seen him was right: there was definitely a fit body underneath that jacket.

'Everything is okay?' he asked, snapping me from my thoughts.

'Yep. Time's ticking, so let's start with something easy: Christmas dinner. Follow me.'

We walked for a few minutes, then stopped outside a coffee shop. As we stepped inside, Nicolas frowned.

'We come for coffee? That is not on the list.'

'Nope, but Christmas dinner is. We won't have time to have a proper sit-down meal, but Christmas sandwiches are very traditional here. And this one has turkey, cranberry sauce, gravy and cabbage—all stuff that's pretty typical to eat for Christmas dinner.' I paid for two sandwiches to take away. When we left the shop, I handed one to him.

'This is a joke, yes?' Nicolas's face crumpled.

'No. Look, you had Christmas dinner on your list and this is a Christmas dinner sandwich. It's as close to the real thing as you're going to get given our time constraints.'

'A sandwich?' he repeated. 'For *dinner*?' He muttered some stuff in French that I didn't understand. Didn't sound like he was happy.

'Are you always this ungrateful?' I hissed.

'I am not ungrateful, it is just I prefer *real* food...'

'Oh, I see. You're a food snob.'

'I hope I am not. I eat baguettes, of course, but... not for dinner.'

'Well, that's what you're getting tonight, so eat up.'

Nicolas unwrapped the sandwich and took a bite.

'It is not horrible...'

'Told you. So, I thought we could go to Winter Wonderland at Hyde Park. Then you can tick at least three things off your list straight away.'

'*Bien.*'

We headed back towards Regent Street. If we crossed over to Hanover Square and then Brook Street, we could walk all the way down to Hyde Park and avoid most of the crowds.

'This way.' I led him across the road.

I felt my phone vibrating and pulled it out. Not again. It was Spencer. There was no point in answering right now. In forty-five minutes I should know whether or not I could get the dryer, so it was better if I spoke to him then.

I couldn't ignore him completely, though—otherwise he'd just keep calling. I typed out a quick text letting him know that I was on the case, committed to finding the gift tonight, and I would update him in approximately two hours. I thought it was better to give myself some leeway. If I said forty-five minutes, then he'd hold me to it and start chasing me again.

I deserved a medal for putting up with him. I really needed to look for another job. But it wouldn't be easy for someone like me.

I hadn't done very well at school or gone to uni, so it was probably harder to get another role. There was so much competition these days. And even if I did find one somewhere, what if I jumped from the frying pan into the fire? Spencer was annoying and condescending, but knowing my luck, my new boss would end up being worse.

'So, Cassie, your boyfriend: he is okay that you spend time showing a Frenchman you have just met around London?'

Boyfriend! As if.

'That was my boss again, not my boyfriend... I don't have one... at the moment...' I tried to make it sound like it was a temporary thing, rather than admitting the fact that I'd been single for a year.

'*Really?*' Nicolas raised his eyebrow. '*Mais pourquoi?*'

'I'm sorry.' I frowned. 'I don't understand.'

'I asked why.'

'Just been busy with work, I suppose.' I shrugged my shoulders. Whilst that was true, it wasn't the main reason I was single.

My phone rang again. Spencer.

'Bloody men!' I snapped, then put my phone on silent. 'If they weren't all such liars and cheats, I wouldn't be in this situation!'

'What?'

'Nothing.' I didn't want to go into it right now. Just thinking about it made my blood boil. 'And you? Is your girlfriend in Paris or will she be joining you in London for Christmas?' I asked quickly to take the spotlight away from me. The less said about my love life or lack of it, the better.

'I do not have a girlfriend.'

No way. How could *he* be single?

'How come? I mean, you must meet loads of women in your job.'

Nicolas laughed.

'*Oui*. I meet lots of women, but I do not want a relationship right now.'

Aha. Knew it. That was his diplomatic way of saying that he liked to play the field.

'So, tell me, is it true what they say about French men?' I turned to face him, ready to see his reaction.

'About us being fantastic lovers?' He grinned mischievously.

'No…' God, he thought a lot of himself. 'I was going to say about them having mistresses and wanting open relationships?'

'*Oui*.' He nodded. 'We also go everywhere with a string of onions around our necks and wear berets every day.'

'Sorry.' I winced. 'I didn't mean to stereotype again. I was just curious.'

'It is okay. I joke with you.'

'Oh.'

'But to answer your question seriously, yes. It is true… Some men have mistress and some married women have lovers. I am sure this happens in England too.'

'Yep. I can definitely confirm that's true…' My voice trailed off.

'Earlier you say that all men are liars and cheats, but that is sexist, *non*?'

'Maybe, but I've got the evidence to prove it,' I added, thinking not just of my cheating boss, but also of my own experiences.

'So if I said *all* women are superficial, or *all* women want only to date men with money, or *all* women are complicated, you would think this is okay?'

'Of course not!'

'So how is what you say about men different?'

'Point taken. Let's just forget about it.' I wanted to get off the subject.

'Fine.' He held up his hands. 'And to answer your other question: if you are really curious to know if French men are good lovers, Cassie, I say that maybe one day you will find out…'

CHAPTER SIX

'This is it,' I said as we arrived at Hyde Park. In the distance I could see the illuminated roller coasters, the big wheel and other funfair rides. My stomach sank as I thought about the last time I came here. Twelve months ago. Back then I hoped that I had a happy Christmas ahead of me. But I was wrong.

'This looks cool.' Nicolas took in the surroundings.

'Yeah… so being here means we get to tick visiting a Christmas market off your list straight away,' I said quickly, eager to focus on the objective and not get lost in my thoughts. 'There's loads of street food stalls and festive bars, so it'll be easy to get some mulled wine. You can go ice-skating too. I reckon you should do that first, because there will be queues.'

'*D'accord.*'

We joined the line for the box office. Although entry to the festival was free, he'd have to pay for his ice-skating ticket.

'Actually…' I rubbed my hands together. They were

freezing. I really wished I hadn't forgotten my gloves. 'Whilst you're queuing, I'm going to find a loo.'

'Loo?' Nicolas frowned.

'Sorry, a toilet.' I should have gone earlier when he had. 'I'll meet you back here, okay?'

'Sure, but one moment...' He took off his gloves. 'Your hands are cold? Take these.'

My stomach flipped. They really were freezing, but I couldn't say yes.

'Thanks, but then *your* hands will be cold.'

'*Ne t'inquiète pas*. Do not worry. Take them. If you refuse, I will be offended and remember you told me that you were not rude.'

'Okay, then.' I took them from him and slid my hands inside. They were lined with sheepskin so were extra warm. Not to mention huge. I could probably get two of my hands inside one glove. 'Thank you.'

'*De rien.*'

I looked around, searching for a toilets sign. I was bursting. Eventually I found the ladies', but of course, there was a queue.

I looked at my watch. Still half an hour until he could call Andrew. I stood behind a group of girls and took a moment to take everything in. This was all kind of nuts. A couple of hours ago I was about to get the tube home for a quiet night in by myself, and yet here I was at Winter Wonderland, a place I thought I'd never visit again, hanging out with a handsome stranger. Oops, I meant *doing a good deed for a stranger*. His appearance had nothing to do with it.

As I looked around, it felt like I was existing in a parallel universe. Everyone around me was happy. Even those queuing in the cold had big smiles on their faces. I guessed Christmas had that effect on people. I used to be like that. Not anymore, though.

Fifteen minutes later, I headed back to the box office, hoping Nicolas was still there. I hadn't expected it would take so long. He probably thought I'd spent all that time in the loo doing a number two.

As I walked towards him, Nicolas's face lit up. Butterflies started dancing in my stomach, which I tried to suppress. It was difficult though. He really was gorgeous, and despite being arrogant, giving me his gloves was a sweet gesture.

'Sorry. There was a massive queue. All done?'

'*Oui*. I have the tickets.'

'Tickets, as in more than one?'

'*Bien sûr*.'

'Oh… you didn't have to buy me one…' I winced. It was kind of him, but I couldn't accept. I hated ice-skating. I didn't want to sound ungrateful, though.

'You do not like?' He read my mind.

'Not really… sorry. Maybe if we go straight back, I can get a refund for my ticket?'

'What is the problem? Why do you not like?'

I sighed. He'd probably think I was a wuss if I told him. Nicolas placed his hand on my shoulder and his body heat sent shockwaves through me. It was like he'd put me under some sort of spell, because before I knew it, I'd opened my mouth and was about to spill my guts.

'I used to go. When I was a teenager. But the last time I went, a man fell on the ice and then someone behind him didn't stop in time and skated over his face. There was blood all over the rink. It was awful.' The image flashed into my head and I instantly felt sick.

'*Mon Dieu*. That must have been terrible. But, Cassie, these things: they happen. You cannot let fear stop you from enjoying life, *non*? This was a long time ago. Let us try again tonight. I will help you.'

I looked at my watch.

'And then there's the dryer. You need to call Andrew back soon, so I don't have enough time anyway.'

'Yes.' He bowed his head. 'That is true. I am sure he will have it, though. So when he has sent it to your boss, you can skate then, yes?'

If he found this for me, it would be a weight lifted off my shoulders, so a few minutes of ice-skating would be a small price to pay.

'Okay…'

'*Genial!* It will be fun. Just like Christmas should be.'

'Yeah, about that… just a heads-up that if I'm not that enthusiastic about everything here, it's because Christmas isn't really a favourite time of year for me.'

'*Non? Pourquoi?*'

I took a deep breath. Was I really ready to go into this now? He was still a stranger and it was kind of embarrassing.

'Let's go and look around the Christmas markets. We can tick some things off your list whilst we're waiting to make the call.' I quickly changed the subject. I wished I hadn't brought it up at all, but I wasn't good at acting and sooner or later he'd notice my lack of excitement.

We strolled through the traditional German Christmas market. There were loads of cute chalets, overflowing with festive goods. We passed a stand selling gloves and Nicolas insisted on buying me a pair.

'Honestly, you don't have to. I have a pair at home but just forgot them.'

'Do not worry. I offer not because I am nice. It is just because my hands are cold. If I buy these for you, you give my gloves back to me. You see? You were right. I am dickhead.'

'I knew it!' I laughed. 'Okay, then. I will accept your horrible selfish gesture.'

'*Bien.*' He handed the money to the lady, who, of course, fluttered her eyelashes at him, then gave the green leather gloves to me. 'Now, Strawberry, you have the gloves to match your hat…'

I narrowed my eyes but this time didn't protest at the use of his nickname. He was right. The gloves went perfectly.

'*Merci,*' I said as we continued walking. We stopped at one of the bars to buy some mulled wine. Another point ticked off the list.

'So what will you do for Christmas?' Nicolas took a dark hat from his pocket and pulled it onto his head. Didn't blame him, it really was cold. 'You stay with your family?'

'Nope. Not this year. I plan to spend it at home, alone. I'm going to eat whatever I want and enjoy crappy films without having to debate for hours about what to watch.'

Even at this age, whenever I went to my parents' for Christmas, there were always arguments about who got the most roast potatoes or a battle for the remote control.

At first, my parents had been upset that I wasn't coming this year, but my two sisters weren't going either and my brother had bailed too. Then Mum had decided it would be nice for her and Dad to visit her family in St Lucia, so it was all sorted. They'd have a lovely time in the sunshine and I'd have a nice time chilling at home.

'It'll be great!' I continued. 'I can just sit there all day in my onesie, snuggled up on the sofa with my colouring books, and switch off from the world.'

Nicolas laughed. *Not him as well*. Ever since one of the guys at work had caught me colouring in my lunch break, I'd got so much stick about it. They kept teasing me, saying it was for kids. But it wasn't. I found it relaxing. It was nothing to be ashamed of.

'I should've known you wouldn't understand.' My jaw tightened. 'I'm talking about *adult* colouring books, not the ones for children. And even if I was, so what?'

'I was not laughing because you said that you colour. I laugh because it is funny—I enjoy colouring too.'

'What?'

'It is relaxing. It helps me to forget about everything.'

No way. I'd never met a guy who liked colouring books. I still wasn't sure he wasn't winding me up, but I'd give him the benefit of the doubt.

'Exactly,' I added. 'I've done it for a few years now. My job is stressful and it helps to calm me down.'

'This is true. You know that some psychologists and therapists prescribe adult colouring books to patients to help with anxiety?'

'Seriously?' My eyes widened.

'*Oui*. It is good for you. It gives the mind good chemicals. Some people may not think it is very macho, but I do not care. Man need something for stress just like woman. For me it is also good for creativity.' Nicolas took a sip of his mulled wine. '*Putain!*' He grimaced. 'This is not for me. Too sweet.'

Although he wasn't convinced by the taste, I enjoyed the sensation of the warm liquid slipping down my throat. It was getting colder, so something hot was exactly what I needed.

'Considering all the donuts you bought earlier, I thought you'd love sweet stuff.' I raised my eyebrow.

'They were not for me…'

I guessed that as there were two coffee cups, he'd bought them to share with someone else. Perhaps another woman? My overactive imagination wondered whether he'd enjoyed some *afternoon delight* with a lady and then taken the coffee and donuts back to his hotel afterwards. Who knew?

'And you? What are your plans for Christmas? What made you come to London?'

'I just want a change. To get away from… just from life…' His voice trailed off.

'Sounds heavy.'

'At this time of year there is a lot of party with people who are not… how do you say when they are not real? They are not genuine?'

'Fake? Shallow?'

'*Voilà, c'est ça*: fake. I do not like to be with these people. And it is a busy time and I want… just to have a quiet time. Do simple things.'

I was definitely in agreement with him on that. I hated snooty people. There were a lot of them at work. With their fancy clothes, expensive watches, flashy cars and huge houses. Always looking down on me like I was nothing more than Spencer's glorified slave.

And this year I was all about having some peace and quiet. I was surprised Nicolas was even allowed time off from working at a salon, though. Must be loads of people needing to get their hair done for fancy functions.

'You still have not told me why you do not like Christmas,' Nicolas added.

'I haven't always hated Christmas...,' I said before I realised I'd opened my mouth. Maybe the alcohol in the mulled wine was helping to loosen my tongue. *Sod it*. I might as well tell him. 'It's just never been a lucky time for me. Even when I was a child.'

'What happened?'

'Where do I even start? Okay, there was one year, can't remember how old I was, but I was an angel in the school nativity play. It was all going well until I had a really heavy nosebleed. The blood dripped all over my white outfit and it was so bad that the boy who was Joseph fainted because he thought I was dying and they had to stop the play to clean up the blood on the stage. The whole thing was ruined.'

'So you do not like Christmas because of a play thirty years ago?' Nicolas frowned. 'That is stupid!'

'Not quite thirty years ago. I'm not that old!'

'How old are you?'

'A gentleman never asks how old a lady is.'

'But according to you, I am not a gentleman, remember?' Nicolas's mouth twitched.

'True.' I smirked. Oh what the hell. It didn't matter if he knew my age. 'I'm thirty-five. You?'

'You do not look it.' His eyes widened and my stomach did that silly dancing thing again. I wished it would calm down. 'I am thirty-seven,' Nicolas added. He didn't look his age either.

'But, anyway,' I went on, continuing the story to avoid staring at him and wondering how one man could be given so many good genes, 'it wasn't just what happened at the play. When I was seventeen, I was working in a shop on Christmas Eve and stupidly tried to break up a fight between two customers wrestling over the last bottle of perfume, and I ended up getting punched in the face. I then spent the whole Christmas holidays explaining why I had a black eye.'

'*Merde*.' He winced.

'That wasn't the only eye-related Christmas disaster. About four years ago my boss asked me to decorate a real Christmas tree in his office and when I was cutting the netting, one of the branches flew into my eye. It was so painful and I couldn't see properly. When I went to the hospital, they said it'd scratched my cornea.'

'*Merde*,' Nicolas repeated.

'Yep. That means *shit*, right?'

'*Oui*.' He nodded. Funny how I remembered French swear words.

'Anyway, eventually it got better. Then there was the Christmas I went to meet my boyfriend's parents for the first time, and to impress his mum I bought her a present. He'd suggested I get her a slim flask, because she wanted something small to take on her walks, but when she opened it, the blood drained from her face. It was only after she dropped it on the floor in horror that I and his entire family saw why. Because the sizes of the boxes were so similar, when I'd wrapped the presents, I got them mixed up, so I'd accidently given her the vibrator I'd bought for my friend Melody.'

'*Mon Dieu!*' Nicolas doubled over with laughter.

'It's not funny! It was embarrassing!'

'No, you are right. It is not funny. It is hilarious! I imagine this was her favourite present!'

'And then last Christmas, my boyfriend dumped... I mean, broke up with me.'

Nicolas's mouth fell open.

'*Connard!* You were with him for a long time?'

'Almost two years. I thought, you know, that we were ready to move to the next stage. We'd come here to Winter Wonderland a few days before and we'd been talking about the future. Finally moving in together, settling down. I'd wanted to for ages, but he was never keen. And then on Christmas morning, just as I was getting ready to go and see my parents, he messaged to tell me it was over.'

'He did not even call you?'

'Nope. Dumped by text. Classy.'

I could still remember it like it was yesterday. At the time, it had felt like it came out of nowhere. How could we go from discussing the future to ending things? It just didn't make sense.

When Jasper eventually had the guts to speak to me on the phone, he said we didn't have enough in common, which I took to mean his family had money and mine didn't, so they all thought we were beneath them.

That was always my concern when we'd first met at a work do, which was the only time I ever met rich people. I never mixed in those kinds of circles, so I didn't see how we'd be able to make it work, and I was right.

If that wasn't bad enough, I heard a few weeks later

that he'd been seeing another woman behind my back. For months, apparently. Just like Spencer, he was a cheat. I think they were engaged now. She was *Lady* something or other. Could be Lady Penelope for all I cared. And they'd moved in together. Turned out it wasn't that he was afraid of settling down. Just settling down with me.

'I cannot believe it.' Nicolas shook his head.

'Then I had to spend the day with my family, especially my parents, asking why he hadn't come with me and when we were going to get married and have kids. It was mortifying. At the time I was too embarrassed to tell them what had really happened—I was still trying to process it myself. So I said he wasn't feeling well. I just wanted to go home and hide under the covers. But instead, I had to spend the whole day with them. It was awful. And so Christmas just reminds me of that now.'

My stomach sank. Even one year on, talking about it was still painful. It still brought back the feelings of not being good enough.

I considered adding the fact that those weren't the only examples of my misfortune during this season, but then decided against it. What had happened the year before last was a mental image of me I definitely did not want a hot guy like him to imagine.

You see, that was when I'd got food poisoning on Christmas Eve and spent the whole night on the toilet. It wasn't pretty. Then I still had to drag my arse to my parents' the next morning, try and be sociable and attempt to keep some food down.

I'd also been dumped on Christmas Day in my early twenties. My boyfriend at the time wasn't replying to the texts I'd sent wishing him merry Christmas and asking if he liked his present. So several hours later I called to check he was okay. Then he told me he wanted to end things. He tried to make it better by saying he'd been planning to wait until Boxing Day. Arsehole. Wish he'd at least done it before I'd wasted money on his gift.

A guy breaking up with me during the festive season, not just once but twice, along with the string of other incidents over the years made it very clear: Christmas was cursed. That was why I'd decided to swear off it for life. If I just kept myself to myself, then nothing bad could happen.

'I am sorry.' Nicolas rested his hand on my shoulder again, which somehow eased the ache in my heart a little. 'And now I make you come to this place and take me to see Christmas things.' He shook his head.

'It's okay. You didn't know. And you didn't *make* me do anything. We agreed to help each other.'

'Well, if you want to leave, I understand.'

'Honestly, it's fine.' I didn't want to admit it to Nicolas, but being here with him wasn't so bad.

'*Merci*. I promise that by the end of tonight, I will make you fall in love with Christmas again.'

'That's sweet, but I don't think that will happen. It's okay, though. I'm just doing this whole Christmas tour guide thing to strengthen Anglo-French relations.'

'So you show me around, just to help a poor French tourist?' He smirked.

'Yep. To prove that British people are friendly and helpful. That's the only reason...' I grinned. *And because you're quite possibly the sexiest man I've ever met.*

'And to get the dryer for your boss...'

'Oh shit!' I looked at my watch. We should've called Andrew half an hour ago.

'Do not worry. I will call him again. He must be there now.'

I really hoped so. The shops would be closing in less than half an hour, so if he couldn't get it, I'd be screwed.

CHAPTER SEVEN

It was the moment of truth. I was about to find out whether I was really going to get this godforsaken gift or if Nicolas had been spinning me BS for the last couple of hours.

I watched the people going round and round on the big wheel as Nicolas paced up and down several metres away on the phone. The call was lasting a lot longer than the previous ones, so maybe that was a good sign?

When I'd handed Nicolas the phone, I'd noticed that Spencer had called. One way or the other, as soon as Nicolas gave me the verdict I'd need to update him straight away—otherwise, all hell would break loose.

Nicolas walked over, his face emotionless.

'So?' I said quickly.

'I am very sorry Cassie, but…'

'It's okay. I knew it was a long shot, but thanks for trying anyway.' God only knew how I was going to find the gift now.

'You did not let me finish. I want to say that I am very

sorry but Andrew cannot get the dryer to you tonight. His taxi company has no one to collect it. But he can get it there in the morning.'

'What? So he's got one?' My heart skipped a beat.

'*Oui*. I told you he would.'

'Seriously?'

'What is wrong with you, woman?' Nicolas frowned. 'Do you not understand English or simple French? I said *oui*: that means *yes*, he has it.'

'Thank goodness!' I threw my arms around Nicolas's neck. God, he smelt so good. All woody and manly. And his hair had the most delicious scent. I couldn't quite work out the fragrance of his shampoo, but it was divine. I was about to sniff it again, then I came to my senses. *WTF*. I quickly stepped away. 'Sorry.' I cringed. 'Didn't mean to hug you. I'm just so relieved!'

'It is okay. I told you I would help you find it.'

'Is Andrew staying in the salon for a bit longer?'

'Yes, I think so.'

'Well, would you mind if I got one of my own couriers to collect it? Then I'd know it's done and I can relax.'

'I am sure that will be fine.'

'Brilliant! And I can give him the company credit card details over the phone to pay for it.'

'I think he cannot take payments now because the reception lady has gone home.'

'Okay, well, if you trust me, I can call and do it tomorrow. Whatever you need.'

My heart soared. I felt like a fifty-tonne weight had been lifted from my shoulders. I'd found the dryer. *Thank God.* Then reality hit me and I told myself not to get too excited just yet. Maybe I should hold off from popping the celebratory champagne until I had confirmation that it had arrived safely. I was close, but I wasn't completely in the clear yet.

I quickly called our courier company and gave them the address of the salon, which I found online. Luckily I was able to order a priority bike to collect the package straight away, so they would pick it up within the next twenty minutes, then take it straight to the office. Spencer had been very clear in his reply to my text that it absolutely could *not* go to his house. The last thing he wanted was for his wife to see that he'd ordered another one. Made me feel so sick that he'd dragged me into his sordid mess.

I'd asked the courier company to let me know when the package had been collected from the salon and when it'd been delivered. Then Christie, one of the other PAs at the firm who always worked late, would take a photo of what was inside the box and send it to both me and Spencer, just to be one hundred percent sure that it had arrived. It would then be locked away until tomorrow morning, when she'd hand it over to him personally.

It was like organising a military operation. I was used to planning things meticulously, though. I always tried to think of every possible eventuality. Considering what could go wrong so it could be avoided. That was where my overthinking was actually useful.

Crazy that we had to go to such extreme lengths just for a bloody hairdryer. But after all the stress of trying to find one in the first place, there was no way I was going to risk anything happening to it.

'Everything is fine?' Nicolas had just come back from

exploring more of the markets whilst I'd been stood here trying to organise things.

'Should be. Just waiting for the courier company to confirm they've collected it. Hold on…' I glanced at my phone. 'That's them now.' I opened the text message. 'They've picked it up and the driver is on his way to the office.'

I quickly texted both Spencer and Christie to let them know. *Phew. One step closer.*

'*Parfait!*' Nicolas smiled and my stomach flipped. I'd noticed it had been doing a lot of that since we'd arrived at Winter Wonderland and I needed to get it under control. 'So now that you have the dryer, you can ice-skate with me, yes?'

'We're not quite over the finish line yet.'

'*Comment?*'

'Sorry, I meant, although they've collected the dryer, I can't relax properly until I know it's safely at the office and locked away.'

'So you break our agreement?'

'No, but…'

'But what? You said that when the dryer is sent to your boss, you will skate, *non*? And now you say you will not?'

He had a point. I had agreed. I couldn't go back on my word now. He really had saved my skin.

'Okay. A deal's a deal.' I strained a smile.

'*Bien.* Let us go.'

The closer we got to the ice rink, the more my stomach sank. I was looking forward to this about as much as a root canal. Knowing my luck at Christmas, I'd probably slip on the ice and crack my head open or something. Doing risky things was bad enough at the best of times, but at this time of year the chances of things going wrong seemed to multiply.

Okay, maybe I had been lucky to find the dryer this evening, but I wouldn't be surprised if that was where my luck ended. I shuddered, thinking of all the other things that could go wrong. It could arrive at the office, but then get stolen. Or Christie could open the box and discover it was just stuffed with paper. *Oh gosh.* I should've asked the courier to open the box and check it. Shit.

'Ready?' Nicolas asked.

My mind was whizzing at a million miles an hour, worrying about a load of different scenarios.

'Not really.'

'You still worry about the dryer? You worry that something will happen? Come. Let us skate. When you are on the ice you will forget about everything. And when we finish, the dryer will be at the office. It will be fine, Cassie.'

There went that sexy accent again. I just loved the way he pronounced my name. I looked into his hypnotic dark eyes and knew there was no way I could refuse.

'Okay.' He held out his hand and I took it reluctantly. The heat radiated through his thick black leather gloves. Just like when he'd touched my shoulder earlier, I felt sparks firing around my body. It was probably just the gratitude. I was just feeling happy and relieved that despite the odds, I'd tracked down the present. I pushed the thoughts out of my head and focused on the fact that I was about to go skating. If that wasn't a mood killer, I didn't know what was.

I stepped out on to the ice. The rink was set around a Victorian bandstand and glittered with thousands of sparkling Christmas lights. I remembered reading that this was the largest outdoor rink in the UK and I could see how that was true. It felt really daunting.

When it dawned on me that I was here, with my skates on, I started to wobble and almost lost my balance. Nicolas quickly grabbed my arm to help steady me.

'Do not worry. Just hold on to me and you will be fine.'

Well, *that* was an incentive. An incentive not to hurt myself is what I meant. Obviously I wasn't referring to anything romantic…

Even though Nicolas wasn't as awful as I'd first believed—he'd helped me save my job and was very nice to look at—it didn't mean I was thinking about whether anything could happen between us. And even if I was, which, just to clarify once more, I definitely was *not*, like me, he'd also said he wasn't looking for a relationship. So that was that. Other people might be able to handle one-night stands, which was totally cool for them—but it wasn't for me.

'Okay… thanks.' I made a mental note to avoid looking at him as much as possible. Every time I did, I got an annoying fluttery feeling in my stomach.

Nicolas put his arm around my waist and suddenly it was like my body had been set on fire. *Jesus*. His gorgeous woody scent flooded my nostrils and my knees wobbled again. The idea of being on the ice was challenging enough. How the hell was I going to concentrate on keeping my balance and skate at the same time when he was so close to me?

We started going around the rink slowly.

'Relax…,' Nicolas said gently. 'It is okay.' *Easier said*

than done. On the one hand his voice was soothing and calm, but on the other, that damn accent…

I took a deep breath and attempted to go with the flow. After we'd been around the rink a couple of times, I started to relax a little more and I had a good word with myself.

The gift was on its way to the office, so there was nothing more I could do about it now. Worrying wouldn't make the situation any better. As for my fear of being on the ice, I was sure I'd be fine too. Loads of people skated all the time and how many got hurt? Probably a percentage that was too small to count. Just because that man had got injured, didn't mean I would.

I looked ahead of me. There were people of all ages and abilities skating. Kids, people our age and much older. Although there were some pros spinning, hopping and twirling, the majority were just taking it easy. If they could do this, so could I.

Several laps later, I loosened up. It wasn't so bad. In fact, I reckoned it was time to shed the safety blanket. Prove to myself that I could do it.

'I'm going to try and skate on my own now.' I cautiously turned my head to the left. Nicolas had suggested I might feel more comfortable if I skated on the outside, so I could hold onto the barrier if I needed to.

'*Bien!* I will be right here beside you.' Nicolas rubbed my shoulder and my body sparked again. 'There is no need to be afraid. If you fall, which you will not, I will catch you. Okay?'

There went the tingles again.

'That's really kind, thanks.'

I took a deep breath and continued gliding across the ice.

Come on, Cassie. Don't make a fool of yourself. You've got this.

Live music played from the bandstand, and once I started humming along and stopped worrying, I realised I was enjoying myself.

True to his word, Nicolas skated right beside me. With every lap of the rink I completed, I grew more confident. I could tell he was a good skater and felt like, by letting him babysit me like this and stay by my side, I was holding him back.

'If you want to go and have a proper skate, it's okay. I'm fine now.'

'I promised to stay beside you, so I will.'

'Honestly—I'm good. Go and do your thing. Show us Brits how it's done!'

'Well, if you say it like that…' He grinned and sped off across the ice. Nicolas did a little jump and twirled on his heels to face me and wave. Wow, he really *was* good. I could tell he was in his element. Like he'd been set free.

The more I skated, the more I understood how he felt. Gliding across the ice did give you a kind of high.

Every five minutes or so, Nicolas would come back to check on me. We'd go around the rink for a bit side-by-side, then I'd encourage him to go off and do his fancy skating. But when he saw that we only had fifteen minutes left, he insisted that we skate around together.

Nicolas asked for my phone, and this time, I handed it straight over.

'This is a proud moment, *non*? You have faced a fear. You should have a photo,' he said. 'It will be a souvenir of your time on the ice.' But he didn't just take a photo of me. Somehow he managed to continue skating and take a selfie of us at the same time. 'Later you take my number and you send these to me, okay?'

'Course!' I smiled. I was desperate to have a look at the photo, but I didn't want to push my luck. I'd done a good job of staying upright, so it would be silly to try and start scrolling through pictures now.

Before I knew it, our fifty-minute session was up.

'I did it!' I said as we skated towards the exit.

'I knew you could.' Nicolas squeezed my hand. 'I hope that now when you think of ice-skating, you will think happy thoughts.'

'I think I will. I'm pretty proud of myself. Like you said, I faced a fear and I didn't even fall over once.'

'No, you did not. You were very good!'

'Thanks!' I beamed.

Just as I stepped forward, suddenly I lost my footing, slipped and fell, pulling Nicolas down with me.

Me and my big mouth.

I landed on top of Nicolas and almost ended up head-butting him. I could smell his delicious scent again. My heart pounded through my chest and we were so close that I could feel his heart beating too.

Right then and there I wanted to place my lips on his. To taste him. His dark eyes met mine. We stared at each other in silence. God, he was so beautiful. I might be dreaming, but I was pretty sure he was looking like he wanted me too.

He lifted his head and moved it closer. Our faces were now just millimetres apart and my whole body pulsed with desire. It was happening, our lips were about to touch.

'Need a hand, love?' a stocky guy shouted as he reached out his arm. 'You went down pretty hard there.'

Noooooo!

Couldn't he see that we were having a moment?

Actually, no. What was I thinking? This couldn't happen. Thank God he'd come along when he had.

I pulled back from Nicolas and turned to the man.

'That's really kind, thank you…'

'Here you go.' He grabbed my arm and hoisted me up. 'That's one of you back on two feet, now it's your turn.' He reached out to Nicolas. 'Take my hand, mate.'

'*Merci*,' he said politely.

'No worries! That's my good Christmas deed done for the day!' He grinned proudly. 'Better go. More people to rescue!' He chuckled as he skated off.

Nicolas and I looked at each other and burst out laughing. We brushed ourselves off and stepped onto the grass outside of the rink.

'Well, that was fun.'

'It was. Especially when we fall down.' He smirked.

'Yeah, me tempting fate, saying I hadn't fallen over. That'll teach me!'

Although of course it was good that the man had interrupted us when he had, I couldn't help but wonder what would have happened if he hadn't…

CHAPTER EIGHT

B*rilliant!*
       I'd just finished speaking to Christie and she'd confirmed that the box had arrived and it definitely contained the hairdryer. We'd even FaceTimed so I could see her unboxing it and then locking it away.

The word *relief* didn't even begin to cover it. I felt so light. Like the feeling you get after you've struggled home with several bags of heavy shopping and you finally get to put them down. This was fantastic!

I called Spencer, but it went to voicemail, so I left a message to let him know it was all sorted. I didn't expect him to call back and thank me for saving his neck on my day off, but at least I got to keep my job, which was something at least.

'So I guess I'd better get home.' My stomach sank.

'You are leaving?' Nicolas's face fell.

'Well, you've visited a Christmas market, gone ice-skating, drunk mulled wine… and I've stayed a lot longer than an hour, so…'

'That is a shame. I hoped you could help with the rest of my list. But if you have other plans, I understand.'

Plans? If I went home now, the only plans I'd have would be to curl up with my old friends Ben & Jerry. And seeing as I'd be spending a lot of time on the sofa with a tub of ice cream over Christmas, it was hardly a pressing engagement. I'd much rather help Nicolas.

Now that I thought about it, staying out a bit longer to help him was a good idea for multiple reasons. Firstly, I needed to do something to balance out the guilt I felt about enabling Spencer's awful actions.

Secondly, although I was sure that if he really wanted company there'd be a queue of women longer than at the Harrods sale ready to assist, for whatever reason, Nicolas was alone in a foreign country at Christmas, which couldn't be easy. It was one thing choosing to spend it alone like I was, but it was completely different to find yourself here with nobody to hang out with. Yes. Helping was the right thing to do.

'Let me look at your list again?'

Nicolas took it out from his pocket and passed it to me.

'So you've only got a few more tasks left: going to a Christmas party, seeing the London skyline and...' My voice trailed off as my eyes looked at point number ten.

Enjoy a kiss under the mistletoe.

Having the chance to kiss a sexy Frenchman like Nicolas?

Maybe... We'd come so close on the ice.

I know I'd sworn off anything happening before, but it would just be one kiss. That was completely different to having sex. A little smooch was harmless. We were strangers who barely liked each other, so it'd probably just be a little polite peck anyway. I'd be able to get over that in no time.

'And… it's okay.' I snapped myself out of my thoughts. 'I did have plans, but it's fine. I'm all yours for the night!'

I instantly cringed inside. That made me sound like an escort. I was really out of practice with this men stuff. I really wished I didn't put my foot in my mouth sometimes.

'I like the sound of that…' Nicolas smirked.

Was he… flirting with me? For a second I could have sworn I felt a little spark. Could just be my imagination or wishful thinking, though.

'I think we should start with the party.' If I was cool, I would've come up with something to keep the flirting going, but nope. *Sigh.*

'You know how we can do this?'

'Yep!' I smiled. 'We can find a flashy rooftop bar. There's bound to be someone having some kind of Christmas celebration,' I said as we headed towards Hyde Park Corner tube station.

One of the things about being a PA for a rich boss like mine was that I spent a lot of time making reservations at fancy restaurants so that he could wine and dine his clients. Even though I'd never been to those kinds of places myself, I knew where to find them.

'*Bonne idée.* So where are we going?'

'Vista London—it's a rooftop bar on the South Bank. It'd take us ages to walk all the way, though, so we can get the tube to Waterloo and then it's probably about a twenty-five-minute walk from there.'

'Maybe it is easier to get a taxi, *non*?'

'Easier, yeah, but more expensive.' Just as we

approached the tube station, I spotted a homeless man shivering outside with an empty bowl in front of him.

It always broke my heart to see homeless people, but especially at Christmas. I read an article that said that many adults were just a couple of pay cheques away from facing homelessness. It could easily happen to me or someone I knew.

My thoughts then drifted to the people suffering from loneliness. Or who struggled at Christmas because they'd experienced the loss of a loved one or gone through real problems. Not just silly bad luck like I had.

I felt terrible. Here I was happy to be choosing to spend Christmas alone and *not* have turkey with all the trimmings, yet there were so many people like this guy who were alone or homeless who would love the chance to have a family to spend time with and enjoy a big meal. It really put things into perspective.

Before I even realised what I was doing, I reached in my bag, opened my purse, then pulled out a ten-pound note and dropped it into the bowl. I knew it wouldn't transform his fortunes, but it might help him get something warm to eat and drink.

'Thank you, miss!' The man beamed. As we continued walking, I could feel Nicolas's eyes burning into me.

'What?' I snapped. 'I suppose you're going to lecture me about it being wrong to give to the homeless and say it's better to give to charities? I know that it's true, but I can't help it.'

My ex was the same. He always scolded me when I went and bought a stranger a cup of tea or a sandwich or gave them money.

In fact, Jasper was awful. He used to say that it was

their fault that they were homeless and giving them stuff only encouraged them not to fend for themselves. *Ugh.* Easy for someone with money to say that. And he was always rude to shop workers and waiting staff in restaurants. Now that I thought about it, breaking up with him was a blessing. I had no idea how I'd managed to stay with someone like him for so long.

'That is what you think I would say?' Nicolas shook his head. 'I understand why you do it. Most people do not care, but I believe that if you are able to help someone, then you should. I do the same as you.'

'Really?'

'*Oui.* Earlier, when I buy the coffees and donuts in the park, those were not for me. I meet a woman who live on the streets and we talk for a while and I bring her some food—some soup first, then donuts and coffee.'

Fuck. First I'd thought he was a selfish arsehole, jumping the queue, then stuffing his face with a load of donuts, and now I discovered he was actually selfless and doing a good deed to help someone else? I'd got Nicolas so wrong. And I'll admit: the more I got to know him, the more I liked him.

'That's really… nice…'

'It is nothing. Like I said before, Christmas should not just be about making people feel good by buying big things. You can make people happy by giving time, doing something to help them or just being kind, *non*?'

'If only everyone felt that way…' I looked into Nicolas's eyes and nearly melted. It was so refreshing to meet someone who shared my views.

Christmas *shouldn't* be about feeling forced to buy extravagant presents for everyone just to save face and

getting yourself into debt in the process. Sometimes kindness was enough. There wasn't enough empathy in the
world.

'You're full of surprises, aren't you?' I added.

'Why?'

'Well, you're not the rude arsehole I first thought you
were. Deep down, I reckon you're pretty sweet.'

'Sweet? Like that wine earlier? Now you insult me. I
prefer that you think I am dickhead.' He smirked.

'You know what I mean!'

'*Oui*. You are okay too, I suppose. At first I think that
you are just a rude British woman, but you are kind and
cute.'

'*Cute*? What, like a little puppy?'

'Yes, why not?'

'So now you're calling me a dog?'

'No! I did not mean…' Nicolas's face fell.

'I'm only joking! I'll take cute. It's better than
strawberry.'

'Strawberry is one of my favourite fruits, so when I
call you strawberry, it is a compliment.' Nicolas stroked
my cheek gently and held my gaze. As we stood there in
silence, I could feel the electricity sparking between us. I
told myself I should walk away, or at the very least look
away, but I couldn't. It was like he was a magnet and I was
made of steel.

Earlier I hadn't thought he could be interested in me
and I'd dismissed any thoughts that I could be into him,
but somehow, now it felt like something had shifted.

There was no point in denying it anymore: I wished
that we could just skip to point number ten. Having the
chance to kiss Nicolas? *Yes, please. Sign me up.*

'Shall we get the taxi?' Nicolas broke the spell. He stuck his arm out to hail a cab.

Oh.

Looked like I'd misread things. He really wasn't looking for anything. At least not with me.

Gutted.

A taxi indicated, then pulled over. 'This is my challenge and you are helping me, so I will pay for the taxi.' Nicolas opened the passenger door for me and I climbed inside.

As we sat there and chatted easily, I couldn't help noticing again that something had changed.

If we'd taken a taxi together a few hours ago, I was certain that we both would have positioned ourselves at opposite ends of the passenger seat. Maybe I would have deliberately taken my coat off and put it in the centre so we could keep our distance. But now, even though there was still a space between us, I felt drawn to Nicolas. I wanted to whip off the seat belt and sit right beside him. I wanted him to weave his fingers between mine and not let go. In fact, I wanted him to do a lot more than that...

'It is a very beautiful city,' Nicolas said as we drove past Piccadilly Circus and Trafalgar Square before heading along the Thames.

My pulse quickened. Every time he spoke, his accent did all kinds of things to my body. It had been ages since I'd felt those kind of tingles down below or had the *fanny flutters* as my old flatmate Melody would say. And it felt *good.*

'It is,' I said, trying to focus on the sights rather than look into his dreamy, dark eyes. I know I'd said earlier that I didn't want something casual, but as one-sided as it probably was, somehow I felt a connection. It wasn't just his looks. Nicolas wasn't like the other good-looking boys I'd met. He seemed genuine. Kind and caring. And annoyingly, that was a huge turn-on.

'*Merci.*' He took my hand. He'd read my mind. I loved how tactile he was. Touching my shoulder, stroking my back and now resting his big manly palm on mine. If only he knew the effect that was having, though. Every time he was close, my heart raced. And when he touched me, my body went crazy. It was like fireworks had been set off.

'F-for what?' I stuttered.

'For showing me around your city.'

'It's nothing.' I shrugged my shoulders.

'I am grateful, and your kindness will not go unrewarded. I will make sure I find a way to thank you...' His mouth twitched.

'You—you already have by sorting out the hairdryer,' I stuttered again as my mind raced, fantasising about all the things I'd love him to do to me to show his *gratitude*, 'but if you insist, I suppose I could let you...'

CHAPTER NINE

'We're here!' shouted the driver. Nicolas let go of my hand and reached in his pocket for his wallet.

Dammit. Interrupted again. Just when something was *maybe* brewing.

If we'd had a few minutes longer, I might have been able to tell if he liked me or not.

As we approached the bar, there was a group of people leaving, so we were allowed to go straight in. Normally I'd heard this place had long queues. Maybe my luck really was changing tonight. A few people followed behind us as we stepped into the tiny lift.

It was a bit of a tight squeeze, but it would be better than taking the stairs. After showing Nicolas the lights, then walking around Winter Wonderland, plus going ice-skating, my feet were getting tired.

Nicolas slipped at the back of the lift behind me, to make way for a couple at the front. The lift was already packed, so it would have been better if they'd just waited until it came back down again.

The woman looked like she was in her mid-twenties and was dripping in diamonds—diamond earrings, a blinging watch and a huge sparkling necklace. She took her perfectly manicured nail and pressed the button to the top floor reluctantly, like it was covered in shit. She probably wasn't used to having to do things herself.

The short, stocky guy in his late fifties that she was with squeezed up closer to her, but she lifted her head up in the air with disgust and moved away. Maybe they'd had an argument or something. I could definitely feel some tension between them.

Just as the lift began to ascend, it jolted, then stalled. Everyone glared at each other, hoping that the worst hadn't happened.

'What's going on?' Ms Bling said to the guy, like he was some sort of clairvoyant.

'I'm not sure, darling,' he answered in a posh accent. He stretched across her and pushed the button again. Nothing happened.

'Oh God!' she gasped. 'Please don't tell me we're stuck!'

'Press the emergency button,' said one of the girls in front of me. The man pressed it repeatedly. Still nothing.

It was getting hot in here. The girls fanned themselves frantically with their hands and the couple at the front launched into a full-blown argument. I loosened my scarf, took off my coat and held it in front of me.

'It's your fault the lift has broken,' she snapped at him. 'I told you to lose some fucking weight.' I saw his face fall. That was pretty harsh.

'I'm trying, darling.' He bowed his head.

'Well, clearly not hard enough!' she huffed.

'And you say that French people are rude?' Nicolas whispered. He was so close that I could feel his warm breath on my ear, gently tickling my neck and sending shivers down my spine.

'I didn't!' I tried to turn my head to face him, but there wasn't enough room. We were packed into this lift like sardines in a tin. 'I said that's the stereotype. I didn't say I believed it. I mean, yeah, you're pretty rude, but I'm sure not everyone is like *you*.'

'That is true. When you get to know me better, you will see that I really *am* rude... sometimes I have no control over my tongue or my mouth. Especially when I am around a beautiful woman...'

I might be pretty rusty with the whole men thing, but I was pretty sure he was flirting with me, and I liked it. No. I bloody *loved* it. And I reckoned I would love having his rude mouth all over me even more...

Now it was me that needed to fan myself. And not because of the heat coming from all of us being squashed together in this lift.

One of the girls in front of me looked more anxious with every second that passed and her friend tried to reassure her.

Whilst Ms Bling frantically bashed at the lift buttons, I felt surprisingly calm. Surely even if they hadn't heard the emergency bell, someone must realise by now that something was wrong and would be sending help. I hoped so anyway.

The lift jolted and we went flying backwards. I stuck my right hand out to try and steady myself and threw my left hand behind me to hold on to the back of the lift wall.

But then I realised that although it was firm, my hand was definitely not against the wall…

I'd grabbed onto Nicolas's dick.

Shit.

'At least buy me a drink first…' He laughed.

I quickly removed my hand. So embarrassing.

Although it was an honest mistake, I admit, I liked what I felt. Nicolas had a lot going on down there and he felt hard. The thought that there was a possibility that he had a boner because we were so close was a massive turn-on.

'Sorry… I lost my balance and…'

'No need to be sorry. I definitely am not…'

Mmm. So he really was enjoying us getting up close and personal. And the feeling was totally mutual.

Just as I regained my balance, the lift jolted again, pushing me back into Nicolas.

Oh yes…

If I was in any doubt about his levels of arousal, I wasn't anymore. My bum was now pressed firmly against Nicolas's cock and it was definitely feeling like it was happy for me to stay right there.

My heart beat faster and a million naughty thoughts raced through my mind. I wanted to push myself into him. Harder. For Nicolas to rub himself against me.

What was wrong with me? We were in a lift with a bunch of strangers. One couple was having a blazing row and the others looked like they were going to pass out any second.

We were stuck. With no idea when we were going to get out. Now wasn't the time to be thinking about how great it felt to have some sexy French guy's dick against my arse.

I pushed my body forward to try and create some space between us. I didn't get very far because it was so tight in here, but at least I couldn't feel him anymore.

'You do not have to move,' Nicolas whispered, his sweet breath caressing my neck. 'As you can tell, I find you very sexy, Cassie. If you like what you feel behind you, please come closer…'

The moment he said he found me sexy, then said my name, I almost felt the elastic go in my knickers. When we'd first met, I found his directness rude, but now it was a big turn-on.

Nicolas was giving me an invitation: to take things further. But that would be stupid. Irresponsible. As much as I fancied him—and I really, really did and had been fantasising about him ravishing me pretty much the whole night—it was silly to wish that something could happen when it couldn't go anywhere. He'd be leaving tomorrow or on Boxing Day at the latest. He'd said he hadn't decided exactly when yet. But he'd be going back to Paris. To a completely different country, so what would be the point?

Just as my brain whirred, weighing up the pros and cons, I felt Nicolas's hands resting on the side of my waist. His touch set off sparks around my body and tingles between my legs, and before I knew it, my bum was pushing back into him. It was like it had a mind of its own.

Nicolas reciprocated by grinding harder into me.

God, it had been so long.

If these lift doors ever opened, I didn't want to go and look at the skyline. I wanted to go straight back to his hotel…

Nicolas ran his fingers slowly down my outer thigh, then up again, but this time, along my inner thigh.

'Is this okay, Cassie?' he whispered in my ear.

'Yes,' I replied, nodding quickly to make it clear I was enjoying this just as much as he was.

I moved my coat further in front of me to act as a shield and give his hand more room, then parted my legs slightly to make it easier. I was getting wet. His touch was electrifying. If this was how he could make me feel with my clothes on, imagine what he could do when they were off…

Oh God.

His fingers reached between my legs. As he stroked my clit, I threw my head back and a whimper slipped out of me before I could stop it.

Jesus.

That felt so good. Oh, the thrills he could give if he could touch me properly *there*. I wished it wasn't the middle of winter and that I didn't have my jeans on. Winter clothes were so damn restrictive. If it was the height of summer and I was wearing a skirt or floaty dress, he could easily slip his hand underneath and feel me. *All of me.*

As if reading my mind, Nicolas's fingers travelled up further and stopped at the zip on my jeans. He pulled it down slowly, then slipped his hand inside.

Nicolas hadn't even touched my skin yet and I already felt like I was ready to explode.

Just as his hand was about to slide underneath my knickers, the lift plunged downwards and came to a loud halt, then the doors sprung open.

'*Halle-fucking-lujah!*' screamed one of the girls as she

rushed forward. Her friend followed, then collapsed on the floor, gasping for air.

Nicolas quickly slid his fingers out of my jeans.

'Well, get out, then!' Ms Bling scolded as the man stepped through the doors sheepishly. What a bitch.

I felt a draft between my legs. I looked down and saw my zip was still undone. I did it up quickly. I couldn't believe what we'd just been doing.

'Are you okay, miss?' said a guy dressed in a suit. Looked like he was a manager.

'Yeah, fine.' I stepped into the hallway. 'I'm fine.' *Horny and sexually frustrated as hell, but apart from that...* Nicolas followed and stood beside me.

'I am so terribly sorry about that,' suit guy addressed the group. 'There was a slight technical fault, which has never happened before. As soon as we discovered the issue, we tried to rectify it immediately. By way of an apology, we'd like to invite you all to enjoy a complimentary bottle of champagne upstairs.'

The two girls' eyes widened and they instantly recovered from their trauma.

'That's the least you can do,' Ms Bling snapped. 'It better be Dom Perignon!'

I recognised that brand name. It was what Spencer always made me order for his parties. The cheapest bottle was over a hundred pounds. Crikey. I could buy dozens of bottles of Prosecco for that price. Or pay for a couple of weeks of food shopping. I supposed to the super rich, buying a bottle of posh bubbly was the equivalent of a normal person like me buying a can of Coke. It was a completely different world.

'So...' Nicolas stared into my eyes. God, his eyes were

gorgeous. I could get lost in those for days. 'Do you still want to go to the top of the roof or would you prefer we went somewhere else…?'

Somewhere else! Somewhere else! screamed my libido.

But now that very enjoyable moment we'd enjoyed in the lift had passed and I was fully alert again, logical, sensible thinking took over.

'We're so close to completing your list. We'd be crazy to give up now. Might as well go and enjoy a glass or two of champers, take in the views and then, well…'

'And then maybe we can work on the final point: number ten on the list.' Nicolas ran his finger over my lips. 'I hope they have some mistletoe…'

CHAPTER TEN

I was now on my third glass of champagne and it was sliding down my throat a little too easily. It wasn't the brand that Ms Bling had demanded, but I still recognised it as being a pricey one. I had to admit, it did taste nice. Hundreds of pounds a bottle nice, *no*, but I definitely wouldn't turn it down if it was offered to me again. Maybe being in the company of a hot French guy enhanced the experience too.

Nicolas and I had spent the last hour and a bit inside, relaxing on the plush burgundy velvet sofas. This place was just like the photos I'd seen online with a shiny long black marble bar and fancy dimly lit chandeliers.

The décor matched the people here. They were all dressed to the nines. Women with legs as long as giraffes wearing short, sparkly dresses, with full faces of make-up and perfectly blow-dried hair and well-groomed men in expensive suits.

After we'd climbed five flights of stairs and reached

the rooftop bar and I saw everyone here, I almost felt like turning back. I didn't belong in these kinds of places. They made me nervous. Self-conscious. I felt like I stood out like a sore thumb. Like everyone would be staring, wondering what someone like me was doing here. Like they did when I went out with my ex or attended events with my boss. Whenever I was around rich people, I always felt like I was an alien who'd landed the spaceship in the wrong universe.

But then Nicolas had taken my hand and led me to the bar and somehow I felt more relaxed. The manager had arranged for us to sit in a little private area inside and so Nicolas and I sat here joking about all the things that had happened today. Me screaming at him at the donut stand, whose fault it was that we'd kept bumping into each other, how appalling he reckoned it was that I thought a sand-wich could be considered as an acceptable substitute for Christmas dinner, falling over at the end of ice-skating and what had happened when we'd arrived earlier...

Well, we hadn't exactly spoken about what had gone on between us in the lift yet. We'd focused more on the drama with the other people. Every time I thought about it, though, and had flashbacks of Nicolas caressing me *there*, my pulse raced. My mind wandered and naughty thoughts filled my head. I bit my lip, imagining what could have been. Where his fingers would have roamed if we were in there for two minutes longer...

'Shall we go outside and see the views?' Nicolas stood up and offered his hand. I brought myself back to reality.

'Yeah. Almost forgot that's why we're here. Shall we get our coats from the cloakroom?' I paused as we headed towards the outdoor area.

'Not necessary,' Nicolas replied. 'You can find a good place for us outside? I will be two minutes.'

'Okay.' I watched him walk towards the bar, taking in his broad shoulders, solid back and pert bum.

Mmm-mm. So hot.

Not getting our coats might not be such a bad idea after all. It gave me a good opportunity to perv over his body, which was another thing I'd caught myself doing when we were chatting.

Nicolas was wearing a fitted grey polo neck and smart black jeans. I could tell he took care of himself from the way the jumper clung to his chest. I'd put money on there being a pair of solid, muscular arms underneath and a six-pack. And judging by the rod I'd felt pressing against my bum in the lift, his abs weren't the only part of his body where he was packing…

He was right. It wasn't as cold as I thought. The rooftop had outdoor heaters scattered around, which definitely helped. Nicolas headed over to the far end of the deck, then rested against the chrome and glass barrier.

Just as I admired the scenery, a warm hand traced down my back. Nicolas stood beside me and smiled. Holy fuck. He clearly didn't realise what his touch did to me. Or maybe he did…

'Pretty amazing, isn't it?' I said in an attempt to throw cold water over my desire to jump him, which was getting stronger by the second.

'*Oui.*' He nodded, taking in the spectacular views.

'It would look even prettier with snow. But it never snows at Christmas.'

'You do not know that. Perhaps it will this year.'

'Doubt it. It hasn't snowed properly in London at

Christmas for I think about a decade. Maybe even more. Can't remember.' It had threatened to snow a few times this week. Some sleet had fallen this morning but quickly melted. 'Either way, London is beautiful.'

'*Oui*. Almost as good as Paris.'

'Oh, *of course*, you'd have to say that Paris is better.' I rolled my eyes.

'It is true!'

'Is *not*!' I threw my arms up in mock protest. 'London has been voted the best city in the world for something like six consecutive years.'

'Who organised this survey? The mayor of London?' He laughed.

'Very funny.'

'Have you even been to Paris?'

'Nope,' I replied. Truth was, I hadn't travelled that much.

With four kids, my parents hadn't had enough money to take us all on holiday. I remembered we'd gone to St Lucia once when I was younger, to visit my mum's family, but that was about it. Most of my holidays were in the UK. Either going to see my dad's family in Scotland or spending the summer holidays with Bella's parents in Cornwall.

As an adult, I never ventured too far afield either. I didn't know why. I supposed I was always working. Busy making travel arrangements and organising holidays for my boss, but never for myself.

Plus, Jasper, my ex, hadn't been keen on going anywhere far because he said he suffered from travel sickness, so we'd never gone abroad when we were together either. We'd had staycations in the Cotswolds, Cambridge, Bath, that kind of thing, but hadn't ventured any further than that.

'Until you have visited Paris, I cannot accept your one-sided opinion.' Nicolas smirked.

'Fair enough.' I shrugged my shoulders. I would love to go to Paris one day. I was tempted to invite myself to see him there sometime, but decided against it. Didn't want to sound desperate. 'I'm sure Paris is lovely, but so is London. And there must be some things you like about my amazing city. You've chosen to come here on holiday, after all.'

'*Bien sûr*. There are many things I like in London…' Nicolas's eyes darkened, with what I hoped was desire. His gaze raked up and down my body, like he was undressing me. Slowly… He licked his lips and took a step closer towards me. 'London is a city filled with beauty. And I am looking at someone *very* beautiful right now.'

Nicolas lifted my chin. Our faces were now just inches apart and I could feel his sweet warm breath on me. My heart pounded.

'Is that so?' I teased. My body tingled with anticipation. Willing that *this* would be the moment.

'It is. And a beautiful, frustrating, but incredibly sexy woman called Cassie has helped me tick off everything except one thing on my London Christmas wish list. I think it is time that we fixed that…'

Still holding my gaze, Nicolas reached into his pocket, pulled out a sprig of mistletoe, held it above our heads and pushed his lips on to mine. He started to kiss me and the word *passionate* didn't even begin to cover it.

This wasn't one of those limp, polite kisses you saw in cute romantic films. This was burning with pure smoking-hot desire. Nicolas kissed as if we were long-lost lovers who'd been apart for months and had finally been reunited.

His lips coaxed mine apart, hungrily, like I was the only woman who could satisfy his appetite. As his tongue flicked gently against mine, I groaned. *Jesus.* What I was experiencing was French kissing at its finest. I didn't want it to end.

Nicolas tossed the mistletoe on the floor, freeing up both his hands to cup my face.

I pushed my body into his. *Oh God.* His hard-on pressed against my thigh. I wanted him so badly.

He kissed my neck and ran his hands slowly down my back, over my bum, then slid it in between our bodies, brushing gently across my breast.

My knees buckled.

I recovered and I slid my hands underneath his jumper. *Just as I thought: rock-solid abs.* Before I knew it, I was clawing at his belt, desperate to unbuckle it…

OMG.

It was like I'd been possessed by an alternative version of myself who'd conveniently forgotten we were in a public place. As much as I didn't want to, we had to stop. *Dammit.*

I pulled away slowly.

'Mmm…' Nicolas licked his lips. 'That was definitely the most enjoyable part of being in London. So far…'

'We might be in London, but I've definitely enjoyed having a little taste of Paris.' I smirked, wondering whether French kissing was on the national curriculum over there.

Either that or Nicolas had taken advanced lessons. He really was that good.

Tasting his lips made me want more. Now I wanted to find out how it would feel to have that mouth running across my shoulders, circling my nipples, trailing down my stomach and then…

'I am happy to hear that. So now that you have had a little taste, would you like to experience more, somewhere less public?'

My mind raced.

Did I want to? *Absolutely.*

But should I? *Absolutely not.*

As strong as the connection was, I'd only known him for a few hours. It must be approaching midnight now, so I'd met him approximately seven hours ago. That was less than one working day.

Like I'd said in the lift, it would be completely reckless to sleep with him. That wasn't me. I was sensible. I didn't do one-night stands. I never had. I was someone who liked long-term, stable relationships. Nicolas couldn't offer me that.

And if the sex was anywhere near as amazing as his kissing, I'd never recover. I'd be left here in London, pining for a man hundreds of miles away. Sleeping with him would be like taking one bite of the most delicious chocolate cake and then being told I wouldn't be allowed to even finish a single slice.

No.

I'd had a great night tonight. Even better than I could have imagined. I should just call it quits now. Take the memories of this magical day home with me and treasure them. Save myself from the inevitable heartbreak.

Yes, that's exactly what I'm going to…

Nicolas pulled me into him and started kissing my neck.

Oh God.

'*J'ai envie de toi*, Cassie,' Nicolas whispered in my ear. That accent. I had no idea what he said, but it sounded so damn sexy. 'I want you, Cassie…,' he added, clearly sensing I needed a translation.

He'd said my name again. And that he wanted me. I'd tried to resist, but it was too late.

Fuck it.

I'd spent my whole life doing the right thing. Toeing the line. Where had it got me?

After a string of unhappy and unfortunate Christmases, I'd finally been given a chance to enjoy the festive season. I was due some good luck. In fact, I deserved this. I should seize this chance to *get lucky* and enjoy one night of pure unadulterated pleasure.

Just hours ago I'd joked with Santa about having a man to play with, and whether I believed that he'd sent Nicolas to me or not, here he was. Right in front of me. I'd be a fool not to take full advantage. Life was for living, right? A festive fling might be good for me. Help take away the bad memories surrounding this time of year. Help loosen me up. And who knows when I'd get to enjoy a night of passion with a sexy Frenchman again?

'Let's go.' I grabbed his hand and pulled him back inside towards the cloakroom.

'You want to go back to your place? You will be more comfortable there?'

'No. We can go to your hotel,' I said, thinking it would be quicker and maybe safer. At least there'd be some

CCTV to show us going inside if he turned out to be some kind of creep. My gut feeling said he was good. I'd text Bella to let her know where I was, though, just in case…

'*D'accord*—okay.' Nicolas trailed his fingertips slowly across my lips, and this time, I swore I felt the elastic in my knickers snap. 'Tonight whatever the lady wants, the lady will get…'

CHAPTER ELEVEN

W e stumbled out of the taxi. During the journey, we hadn't been able to keep our hands off each other. I couldn't wait to get to his room.

I looked around us. We were back in Green Park, where we'd first bumped into each other.

'Is your hotel far from here?' I wrapped my arm around his waist.

'No, we are very close. Come.' He took my hand and led me under the stone archways and then through a grand doorway.

Hold on.

I looked up at the name on the building and blinked several times. I must be seeing things.

This was his hotel? I followed him inside in a daze.

'Good evening, sir. Have you had a pleasant night?'

'Yes, thank you.' Nicolas smiled.

What. The. Actual. Fuck.

We were at *the Ritz*. You know, as in one of the fanciest hotels in London.

'Erm, Nicolas?' I frowned. 'Is this where you're staying?'

'*Oui*,' he said like it was no big deal.

'But…' I paused. My face was contorting more than an impressionist on *Britain's Got Talent*.

I wanted to say something. I didn't know what exactly. I was confused. He'd said he was a hairdresser, right? I knew there were probably loads of successful hairdressers that could afford to stay in a place like this. Especially the stylists that had their own product ranges, like John Frieda, Nicky Clarke, those kind of people. Or the mega famous ones that styled celebs like the Kardashians or Beyoncé. So was Nicolas a big deal in Paris?

I tried to hide my confusion and distracted myself by taking in the surroundings.

Wow.

I'd never been to the Ritz before, but obviously I'd heard a lot about it. Spencer had been here millions of times. I know his wife liked to meet people here for after-noon tea too.

Right in the centre of the lavish reception area, there was a huge tree—probably about twenty-five feet tall, decorated with massive red velvet bows, giant gold baubles the size of watermelons and sparkling lights.

As we walked along the hallway, I attempted to pick my jaw up off the floor. Everything was so grand. The chandeliers, the abundance of gold decor, the marble pillars… it was a different world.

He took my hand and led me inside the lift. Nicolas quickly helped take my mind off things by kissing me. Feeling his lips on mine made me feel so lightheaded that I was convinced that I could pass out at any second. It was pure bliss.

Nicolas opened the door and we stepped inside.

Holy Mary, Joseph, Jesus and all the freaking wise men.

I felt like I'd just entered Buckingham Palace. This wasn't a hotel room. It was an actual suite. And from what I could see, it was probably twice the size, maybe even three times the size of my flat.

There were floor-to-ceiling windows covered with floral curtains, huge chandeliers, fireplaces and antique furniture.

I removed my gloves and hat as Nicolas led me past what looked like a dining room followed by a living room and study, all the way to the bedroom. I concentrated really hard on keeping my mouth closed, because with every step I took, I was so shocked, it kept falling open.

'So your salon must be pretty popular,' I said, thinking that could be the only explanation.

'Some of my clients have a lot of money and one of them arranged for me to stay here.'

Aha.

That made sense. My boss was always arranging fancy gifts like this for his clients. And actually, now that I thought about it, I remembered my hairdresser saying when she went to New York last year, she only had to pay for her flights because one of her rich clients let her stay in her apartment overlooking Central Park. Lucky thing. Talk about perks of the job.

'You're lucky to have such generous clients.' A suite like this must cost thousands of pounds a night. Jeez.

'*Oui…*' He shrugged his shoulders. 'It is a bit big and

fancy for me. I do not want to talk about work.' Nicolas took off his hat, jacket, gloves and shoes, then stepped forward. He was so close that I could feel the warmth of his sweet breath on my lips. 'I have other, more enjoyable business to take care of. Like kissing every inch of you.'

Hose me down.

After I quickly took off my boots and threw off my coat, Nicolas scooped me up in his arms, carried me over to the grand bed and laid me across it. He climbed up beside me and, before I even had a chance to catch my breath, began kissing me like his life depended on it.

His hands slid underneath my jumper. He pulled it over my head and tossed it on the floor.

Thank God I'd worn decent underwear today. In one swift move, Nicolas unclasped my pink bra, flinging it across the bed.

'*Mon Dieu*,' he whispered. 'You are beautiful.' As he took my nipple in his mouth and started sucking slowly, I whimpered.

'That feels… *so* good.'

'I have not even started yet,' he said before flicking his tongue over the tips of my breasts.

I pulled at his jumper. I wanted to remove it ASAP. I needed to see what was underneath, but at the same time, I didn't want him to stop. It was like Nicolas read my mind, because he paused for a second, whipped it off, then went back to letting his tongue explore my body.

I ran my hands over his broad shoulders and smooth sculpted chest. I couldn't believe my luck. Even if I'd created him myself, I couldn't have asked for a sexier man. His solid abs looked like they belonged on the cover of a men's fitness magazine. *Goddamn.*

My fingers traced the dark hair from his belly button to the top of his jeans. It was like a trail that promised to lead me to the land of orgasms and I couldn't wait to get there.

I tugged at his belt. This time we were alone, so I could go all the way. In between my groans of ecstasy, I undid it quickly, pulled down his zip, then slid his jeans past his glorious arse.

The more he sucked my nipples and caressed my breasts, the more I wanted him.

His hand travelled down to my waist, pulling at my jeans. I unzipped myself, lifted up my bum and dragged them down to my knees.

'I think we are both wearing too many clothes,' Nicolas groaned.

'Agreed.'

We both quickly rolled off our jeans and threw them across the bed. Nicolas climbed on top and started circling my nipples, then kissing my stomach as he slid down my knickers and began stroking me *there*.

'You are so wet, Cassie,' he gasped. I wasn't surprised. I couldn't remember ever being so turned on. '*Je veux te manger.*'

'I don't understand,' I whimpered again.

'I said I want to eat you…'

Holy shit.

Nicolas buried his head between my legs. I gasped sharply as he gently flicked his tongue over my clit. Every stroke felt like lightning sparking around my body.

'I don't know how to say it in French,' I panted, 'but fuck. That feels amazing.' My blood was so hot, I felt it scorching my skin.

I grabbed a fistful of his hair, as Nicolas continued

flicking and sucking, with each movement threatening to tip me over the edge.

'Cassie.' He lifted his head. 'The only French you will need to know tonight is *oui* and *encore*.'

Something told me that I'd definitely be saying yes and asking for more a *lot* tonight. Starting right now…

'*Encore*,' I panted, sliding off his boxer shorts and setting his cock free. It was a sight to behold. Even bigger than I'd imagined when it was pressed against me in the lift, but I was *so* ready. 'Earlier you said whatever I wanted tonight I would get, right?'

'*Oui*.' He stroked between my legs.

'Well, Nicolas,' I demanded, 'I want you inside me. Right now.'

Nicolas reached across the bed, grabbed his jeans, dipped his hand in the pocket, pulled out his wallet and then a condom.

'I like a woman who know what she want.' He licked his lips, ripped the packet and made fast work of sliding on the condom. 'Ready?'

'Yes!'

Nicolas spread my legs then slammed inside me. I gasped loudly, clutching on to the bedsheets.

Whoa. It had been a while.

But it felt fantastic.

We rocked backwards and forwards and I rubbed my hands across his chest. I still couldn't believe this was happening: that less than eight hours ago, I'd planned to go home and just curl up on the sofa, by myself. But now here I was, butt naked on a bed at the bloody Ritz having sex with the hottest guy I'd ever laid eyes on. I had to be dreaming. This was what fantasies were made of. It was insane. In the best possible way. This really was my lucky night.

We'd got into a rhythm and Nicolas had found the perfect spot. I wanted more of him. I needed it deeper.

'Harder.' I dug my nails into his back, pumping my hips in time with his. 'Fuck me harder, Nicolas,' I pleaded as he plunged into me again. I didn't know what had come over me. It must have been all of the pent-up emotions and sexual tension. I'd thought my vibrator was good, but there wasn't an electrical device in the world that could compare to this. This was the real deal. I hadn't got my leg over for twelve long months and now I had a French god on top of me, I intended to make the most of it.

'Oh… *oui.*' I pulled him into me. '*Encore. Encore!* I'm so close.'

'Not yet,' Nicolas panted. 'I want to give you more pleasure. Come. Let me take you in front of the fireplace.' He pulled out and quickly lifted me off the bed and into his muscular arms.

Ooh, yes, please.

I'd never done it on the floor or by a fireplace before. As he carried me across the room, I buried my face into his solid chest. Nicolas's woody scent was intoxicating. I couldn't wait to feel him inside me again.

He eased my legs down to the ground gently, then dragged the duvet off the bed and tossed it in front of the grand white marble fireplace.

'This will make it more comfortable for you.' I lay down across it, drinking in every inch of Nicolas's sculpted body as he towered above me. God, he was magnificent. 'Spread your legs,' he commanded. I opened wider. '*Bien.*'

Nicolas climbed on top and plunged inside me once more. 'Ohhhhh!' I gasped. He thrust harder and harder, then after a few minutes lifted my legs over his head and picked up the pace.

My feet almost caught the edge of the tall freestanding gold lamp which was positioned next to the fireplace. *That was close.* I shifted a little to the right. I wasn't going to let the risk of breaking what was probably an antique spoil my fun.

Nicolas continued pumping in and out, plunging deeper and deeper, then slipped his hand between my legs and started stroking my throbbing clit. *Jesus.* There was no way I was going to be able to hold on much longer now. I raised my hips, pushing against him. My body was sparking so much I was sure it was about to burst into flames.

I'm close. So close. It's going to happen any second.

'I'm coming.' My breathing turned into erratic panting as I felt the wave building and the blood race through my veins.

'We will come together.' He slammed into me over and over, his breath growing heavier with every deep thrust. My toes curled and my body shook repeatedly. I was powerless to stop it. *Game over.*

'*Oui, oui, oui…!!!*' I cried out, grabbing onto his firm arse as I reached the point of no return.

Seconds later, Nicolas groaned, then collapsed on top of me. We both lay there trying to catch our breath.

Holy shit.

Merry early Christmas to me.

That was definitely the best Christmas present I'd ever

had. In fact, hands down the best sex and orgasm I'd ever had.

Up until thirty seconds ago I'd thought all that *let's come together* stuff only happened in books and films. I'd never had it actually happen to me in real life before.

Wow.

Nicolas rolled over beside me. After a few minutes, we turned to face each over.

'So…' He stroked my cheek. 'You think I am like the stereotype? Is this how you imagine French men are in the bedroom?'

'*Oui!*' I said, still catching my breath. 'Even better. This will definitely go a long way with helping Anglo-French relations. Although…' I traced my fingers across his chest. 'It could just be beginner's luck.'

'When it comes to sex, I am certainly no beginner, Cassie, and my performance has nothing to do with luck. But how do you say in English? Action is more powerful than words, *non*…?' He stroked between my legs. 'You will soon discover that I have a lot of energy, so you will not have to wait long before I am ready to give you an *encore*…'

CHAPTER TWELVE

S o *this* was what it felt like after having a one-night stand.

I sat up in the huge bed and stretched my arms up in the air. My cheeks flushed as flashbacks from last night flooded my thoughts.

Oh, the fun we'd had.

Nicolas hadn't disappointed, giving me no less than two encores. It just got better and better. I couldn't get enough of him. I felt so naughty. And sexy. Even though I'd never taken drugs before, this was what I imagined it was like to feel high. It was like I was floating. Talk about kicking off Christmas Eve morning with a bang.

I checked the time on my phone. It was almost nine thirty. I'd had a good lie-in. I tossed the duvet off and got out of bed. *Ouch*. I was still so sore. The pain was a small price to pay for the pleasure, though.

I hobbled over to the sumptuous gold-and-red chairs, picked up the thick, fluffy dressing gown I'd put there after round two and wrapped it around my naked body. I opened the curtains, and wow. The room overlooked Green Park and the views were incredible.

I remembered jokingly wishing for a penthouse over-looking the park yesterday when I'd scoffed about the whole putting things into the universe stuff, but I'd never believed for one second that I'd get to spend the night in one several hours later.

The trees were covered with a light dusting of sleet. It was snowing again, but only lightly. It was a shame it wouldn't settle. Still, it didn't matter—I'd already had the perfect night with Nicolas.

Speaking of the French god, I wasn't sure if Nicolas was here. This suite had so many rooms he could be in any one of them.

I checked the two large marble bathrooms, the two dressing rooms (I know, right? I'd love to have just one of those), the study, then the kitchen and dining room, but he wasn't there.

He'd probably gone for a walk or a run. He looked like he kept fit. We'd exchanged numbers earlier, so I was tempted to text him, but I decided to wait.

My stomach rumbled. I was starving. We'd definitely worked up an appetite last night. I wondered how much it cost to order room service breakfast here. Probably one week's salary. M&S was only across the road—I could just get us some croissants from there.

As I passed the huge living room, I noticed a book on the table. *So cool*, I said to myself as I got closer. It was a colouring book, with freshly sharpened colouring pencils beside it. I couldn't resist flicking through the pages. Inside there were views of different cities. I spotted New York, Tokyo, London and, of course, Paris. Each one had been coloured in perfectly and all within the lines. Nicolas really was into this just as much as I was. I smiled as I put the book back on the table and returned to the bedroom.

Just as I walked in, I heard my phone ping. There was a two-word text from Spencer saying 'Got it', in response to the hairdryer texts I'd sent last night. *Thank God.* Then there was a message from Bella.

Bella

Are you still alive? And did you get lucky…?

Nice of her to check up on me. I laughed at the winking emoji she'd added.

Me

Just about…

Me

And yes I did!! I feel like I've sat on a giant cactus, but it was worth it!

Me

He was A-MAZING! Seriously. I've never experienced anything like it. When I met him, I thought he was a dickhead, but he's actually really sweet.

Bella

By the sounds of things I'm sure you weren't complaining about his d*** last night… Glad you enjoyed yourself, hon.

Me

I definitely wasn't. It was glorious! Still can't believe it! Bumping into a hot guy like him. What are the chances?!

Bella

I know! See what happens when you put things out to the universe!

Me

Normally I don't believe in all that manifesting stuff, but I have to admit, it is all a bit of a coincidence. Don't know whether the universe or that Santa Claus bloke was responsible for this happening, but I'm happy it did!

Me

And I spent the night at the Ritz! You wouldn't believe the size of this suite!

I quickly snapped some selfies in the bedroom so Bella could see the size of the bed, the huge windows and the views, then sent it to her. If Nicolas was here, I'd probably be too embarrassed to do that, but hell, this was a new experience for me. It wasn't every day I got to stay somewhere like this, and it was unlikely to happen again. I needed a memento so that in years to come I could remind myself that this was actually real. It was Christmas Eve and rather than things going wrong like they always did, for once things were finally going my way.

Bella

Wow! Very fancy. You deserve this and more. Christmas has been rubbish for you these past couple of years, so you were due a happy one. Hope your festive spirit has been restored!

It actually had. Seeing the Christmas lights with Nicolas and spending the evening together at Winter Wonderland was really fun. I couldn't remember enjoying myself so much. And, well, the party for two we'd had here last night was the cherry on the top.

Nicolas had promised that he'd make me love Christmas again by the end of the night, and he'd definitely delivered. In more ways than one.

Me

Yep. I'm officially full of festive cheer! Nicolas goes back to Paris today, which is a major bummer, but I'm going to try not to think about that. Hopefully we can spend the day together, but either way, I want to just enjoy the moment.

Bella

Brilliant! Glad to have the old Cassie back!

Me

Less of the old, thank you!

I heard the suite door close.

Me

Better go! He's back!

Bella

Oooh! Enjoy round ten, or whatever number you guys are up to now!

I sent an aubergine followed by a row of love heart emojis, tossed my phone on the bed and hurried out into the hallway to greet Nicolas.

'Ready for an encore?' I called out.

'Who are you?' snapped a tall woman with a thick French accent. She had long, glossy hair and striking full red lips and was wearing a fitted white dress. She had the kind of figure many women dreamed of. Well, I did anyway. Small waist, long legs and pert boobs. She looked expensive, sporting a huge sparkling gold watch on her wrist and carrying what I instantly recognised as a fancy designer bag.

All kinds of thoughts flashed through my mind. Was this her suite? Had Nicolas somehow scammed his way into using it for the night and then left me here high and dry to face the music? No, that couldn't be right. The man at reception yesterday seemed to recognise him.

So if it wasn't that, what was the explanation?

'Well?' she snapped again, putting her hands on her hips.

'I'm a…' I didn't really know what to say. I couldn't exactly say that I was his one-night stand. That would sound so cringey. 'Nicolas invited me…'

'Typical,' she huffed. 'I leave him alone for one night and this happens. Look, I know Nico sees women, but you will not last. They never do.' She pushed past me and walked through to the bedroom, as if she was hoping to find him there. She looked at the unmade bed and huffed again.

'Look. I do not know who you are or what you think you had with Nico last night, but you need to understand that he is a man who appreciates the finer things in life…' She lifted her hand and gestured towards herself from head to toe. 'And judging by those disgusting fake boots over there, that is not you.'

My stomach plummeted.

Hold on. When she lifted her hand, did I see a diamond ring on her wedding finger?

Shit.

Please don't tell me I'd just slept with a married man.

Jesus.

Having a one-night stand was one thing, but screwing another woman's husband was a definite no-no.

I was mortified.

Now I was just like Spencer's mistress, Sally. And that lady, whatever her name was, that Jasper had cheated on me with.

No, no, no!

I should have known someone like him couldn't be single. I'd heard about it being common for French guys to have lovers. I'd even mentioned it yesterday to Nicolas and he'd kind of brushed it off. And now here I was. I'd unwittingly become the other woman.

'I know you are after his money, but you will not get a penny. So I suggest you pack up your cheap clothes and leave.'

'His money?' I frowned. Now I was really confused.

'Oh, do not act innocent,' she hissed. 'We both know that is the only reason you are here. Because you want to spend the night with a handsome millionaire. You have your fun. Now you can leave.'

Millionaire?

What the hell was she talking about?

Either way, I wasn't going to stick around to find out. I knew I didn't belong here. And I knew that Nicolas was too perfect. Who was I kidding thinking someone like him would be interested in me?

It was like a replay of the Jasper situation all over again.

I didn't even know why I was so surprised. It was

Christmas, after all, and that always meant bad luck for me.

What was that saying? *If something is too good to be true, it usually is.* Whoever said it was right. Just a shame I had to find out the hard way.

CHAPTER THIRTEEN

I stormed out of the lift into the grand reception. That was so humiliating.

She'd literally stood there, arms folded, waiting for me to get dressed and get out. After I'd put my clothes on in the bathroom, I'd quickly scooped up my phone, handbag, coat and the rest of my things, then left. That stuck-up cow made me feel so cheap. So worthless. I just wanted to get home, take a long hot shower and wash the morning away.

'Cassie?' I looked up and saw Nicolas walking into the hotel. 'Where are you going?'

The nerve of this guy.

'Shouldn't you be getting back to your *wife*?' I snapped.

'*Comment?* My *what*?' He frowned. 'What are you talking about?'

Unbelievable. Was he really going to deny it?

'I saw her, Nicolas. And the sad thing was, she wasn't even surprised about the fact that you'd spent the night with another woman. *Me*.' I winced. I felt so ashamed.

'Happens quite frequently, apparently, but she was kind enough to reassure me that your flings never last. I mean, I know this was a one-night stand and you said earlier that you weren't looking for a relationship, so you don't owe me anything, but you could have at least been honest. Told me you were married instead of lying about being single and getting me involved in some sordid affair.'

I suddenly noticed that all the guests and hotel staff were rooted to the spot. They looked horrified. One woman in a fur coat gasped loudly and pointed like she'd just seen a ten-foot monster.

I supposed I couldn't blame them. I was airing my dirty laundry not just in public, but in the reception of a posh five-star hotel. My outburst looked and sounded like an episode of some tabloid reality talk show. How had I got myself wrapped up in all this drama?

'Should we go outside or talk about this upstairs?' Nicolas put his hand on my shoulder. I brushed it off.

'Don't touch me! There's nothing to talk about. We had a good time. Let's just leave it at that.'

'I really do not understand.'

'Oh, *please*!' I rolled my eyes, as I stepped outside. God it was freezing.

'Cassie: *s'il te plaît*.' Nicolas followed and grabbed my arm. 'I am confused. Please explain to me what you are talking about.'

'The woman! She came to the room. Your wife. You know: long, glossy dark hair, dripping in expensive clothes, wearing a wedding ring… sounding familiar yet or are you going to continue pretending that you've suddenly developed amnesia?'

'Oh…' The penny had finally dropped. Nicolas looked

at his watch. 'But she is early? I was not expecting her until this afternoon.'

'Is *that* all that you have to say!' My mouth fell to the floor. I was right about him all along. 'You're unbelievable! I knew you were a dick!'

'*Non!* You do not understand. She is not my wife! Yvette is my client. You know, the one I told you about yesterday? The one who organised the room? For me to stay here. I am cutting her hair at two o'clock. That is what we had arranged.'

I paused. Could he be telling the truth? I looked straight into his hypnotic eyes. *Hmmm*. He seemed genuine, but I couldn't be sure. Even though I was annoyed with him, his accent still did funny things to my body, so maybe I wasn't thinking straight. I wished he didn't look hotter than hell. That stubble. Hair I wanted to run my fingers through. And those full lips that had roamed all over my body last night and this morning.

Stop it.

Focus, Cassie. Focus.

'Look!' Nicolas held up a bag. 'I went shopping. For ingredients. Instead of order room service, I want to make you breakfast. One of my special omelettes. You were sleeping and I did not want to wake you to tell you I was going out. I want to surprise you.'

'Well, thanks to your lady friend, you definitely achieved that. If she's not your wife, then there's no way there's nothing going on between you two. She was *not* happy to see me. She practically kicked me out and said things would never work between us because I was basically a pauper and you preferred someone posh like her.'

'*Ce n'est pas vrai!*' He shook his head. 'You have to

believe me. I feel nothing for Yvette. I have done nothing with her. We have not had sex. She is just a client. If you want, we can go to the room now, together, and I can talk to her about this. Make her tell you the truth.'

I sensed he wasn't bluffing. But even if he wasn't lying, I couldn't give him a pass just because he had good morning-after etiquette and said he was going to make me breakfast. That didn't excuse the other stuff he'd hidden from me.

'She said you were rich. Is that true?'

Nicolas squirmed. 'Yes… I have money, but that does not matter.'

'Of course it does! Money always gets in the way of everything. You live in a different world to me. Different lifestyle, different people, different expectations. I know what it's like and I don't belong in your circles. Look. I don't know why I'm even reacting this way. Like I said, this was just a hook-up. You don't owe me anything.'

My stomach plummeted. I knew I shouldn't be upset, but the truth was I was gutted. I knew I wasn't cut out for this one-night stand stuff. Which was why I'd never had one. I developed feelings too easily. I couldn't let him know I was hoping for something more, though. I'd look stupid. One night was what we both signed up for. I had no right to expect anything else.

'But, if you just—'

'It's fine,' I snapped. 'You don't need to take me upstairs to prove that you're not married. That's how these things work, isn't it? No strings, no commitments. What you do with your life is none of my business. We had a great night together, now you'll go back to Paris, I'll go back to my little flat in South London and we'll both slip into our normal routines again like we'd never met. Have a nice life.'

I turned and walked to the tube. I heard Nicolas call out my name, but there was nothing more to say.

Our fun fling was over. Yeah, I'd hoped it could have lasted longer, but even if he was interested, it was obvious that things could never work between us for any real amount of time, so what was the point of prolonging the inevitable?

The tube doors opened. I stepped inside the carriage then plonked myself down on the seat. I bet Nicolas had never even been on a tube before. Or a bus. Like I said, we were from completely different worlds.

He could tell me until he was blue in the face that him being loaded wasn't an issue. But I knew differently. Been there, done that, worn the T-shirt.

Jasper's parents had money and it was always rammed down my throat in one way or another. He liked going to expensive places and I always felt shitty because I could never pay my own way. And his mum constantly looked down on me. Like she wanted better for her son. In her eyes I was just a PA. A glorified skivvy. My mum was a nurse and my dad a builder. To me, they were hardworking, good people, but to her, we were just paupers.

I always dreaded going to dinner at their house or to one of their family gatherings. I worried that I'd use the wrong cutlery or say the wrong thing. It made me shudder just thinking about it.

I couldn't go back to that again. Nicolas lived in a world where spending thousands of pounds just to sleep in a hotel for the evening was normal. That room probably cost more for one night than I earned in two months. Yeah,

I knew that Yvette woman had organised it for him, but from what she said, it didn't seem like Nicolas was short of a few bob, so he could've easily paid for it himself. Either way, I didn't want to be around snooty people who made me feel like I wasn't good enough. I did enough of that every day at work.

And even if he *was* telling the truth about not being involved with Yvette, a miracle happened and I won the lottery so the whole money thing became a non-issue, I still had to remember that Nicolas lived in another country. Hundreds of miles away.

No. It wouldn't work.

Did I regret it? The pain in my heart right now said yes. But if I was being honest, apart from the last hour, the time I'd spent with Nicolas was magical. I didn't think I'd ever be able to forget it, for as long as I lived.

But I had to face facts. It was just a one-off. My one lucky night. Although it was fun whilst it lasted, there was no escaping reality.

It was over.

CHAPTER FOURTEEN

I flopped down on the bed. I'd had a shower and felt a bit better. To be honest, it all still seemed like a dream.

Nicolas had called and texted several times since I'd left him standing outside the hotel. But I hadn't replied. It was better that way. In a couple of hours he would have finished doing his client (possibly in more ways than one) and would be going back to Paris.

It annoyed me how much him leaving bothered me. I mean, I hadn't even known him for twenty-four hours and yet I found myself missing his smile. The way he said *Cass-seeee* in his beautiful accent.

I laughed every time a memory from last night popped into my head. How that guy didn't get that we were having a moment when I fell over on the ice and he interrupted what would have been our first kiss.

I picked up my phone and started scrolling through the photos. Nicolas looked so gorgeous outside Annabel's. His eyes sparkled almost as brightly as the lights.

There were the ones on the ice rink and a couple I'd

taken at the Christmas market too where he'd pulled a funny face. How did he still look good even with his tongue hanging out and his eyes bulging from their sockets?

But it wasn't just his looks. It was the way he made me *feel*. Happy. Comfortable. *Special*. He'd never judged me or made me feel small. I could just be myself.

Even so, having such strong feelings for someone so soon was ridiculous. Hopefully all this pining over him was just a temporary thing. Once I'd got Christmas and New Year's out the way, I'd be back at work and rushed off my feet as always, so that should make it easier to get over him. Yeah. I just needed to get through the next week and a bit, then Nicolas would be a distant memory.

Just as I reached for the body lotion, my phone rang again. This time it wasn't him, it was Bella.

'Hey.' I put her on loudspeaker and pumped some lotion onto my palms.

'Hey you! Still living it up at the Ritz with your hot *monsieur*?'

'Nope.' I filled her in on what had happened.

'I'm so sorry, hon. I really had a good feeling about this one... the way you met and everything, it just seemed like he'd been deliberately sent to you like some sort of special Christmas delivery. Maybe you should try speaking to him?'

'I don't see the point. I'll just try and enjoy the memories and put it down to experience.'

'If that's what you really want...' Bella paused. 'One thing you *mustn't* do, though, is to ever feel like you're not good enough. I hate hearing how you let Spencer and all his stuck-up clients at work and now this Yvette woman get to you. People are still people. Rich or not, they still bleed, throw up and go to the toilet, just like we do, so don't put yourself down and put others on some sort of diamond-encrusted pedestal.'

Deep down, I knew she was right. I was just scarred from past experiences. If I was honest, if Yvette hadn't told me Nicolas was minted, I'd never have known. In the whole time we spent together, he seemed pretty normal. He didn't make a big deal about money. Even when I was bowled over by the room at the Ritz, he just shrugged it off. And he was going to cook me breakfast. That was really sweet. Especially considering it would have been much easier to just order room service or get some croissants from one of the many coffee shops around here.

Maybe he *was* different? Didn't matter now. There were still too many obstacles.

'Yeah. Anyway, let's not talk about him anymore. I need to move on.'

'Fair enough. But remember, it's not easy to meet someone special, so think about giving him a chance to explain properly before you write him off completely. Anyway, the reason I was calling, other than to check that you were still in one piece, of course, was about Paul's present—you know the dancing milkshake. Mike's taken him to the park, so I was wrapping a few last-minute gifts and I realised I didn't have it.'

Seriously? How could I forget something so important? Even though I'd given Bella his main gift last week, I knew this was the one he was really looking forward to opening.

Most kids probably wouldn't think it was anything special. It wasn't this year's hot new game or something that had been advertised everywhere. It was just an old toy from a McDonald's Happy Meal. I used to collect them religiously when I was younger and this one was from the nineties. It had the milkshake cup at the base and then froglike eyes on top of the lid, with a straw coming out of it. It also had a kind of mouth, which was formed by the gap between the lid and the cup, and when you wound it up at the bottom it would 'dance'.

For some reason, Paul had been captivated by it when he'd last come to visit me. Bella said he wouldn't stop talking about it and found it hilarious. He asked if Bella could buy him one, but because it was so old, it wasn't something you could find easily, so I'd put it to one side for him.

'Shit! I'm so sorry. I meant to give it to you before you left, but we got sidetracked talking about what had happened with Father Christmas. I'll come and drop it off this afternoon. I know Paul was really looking forward to opening that present on Christmas Day.'

'You can't get the tube all the way to North London. That'll take ages.'

'It's okay. I don't mind. I don't have any plans for the rest of the day and there's no way I'm going to let Paul down.'

'I feel bad about you trekking over here on Christmas Eve. Once Paul and Mike are back, I could take the car and at least meet you halfway.'

'Don't worry. I'll sort it. I should have remembered to give it to you yesterday. I'll make sure that you get it so it can be under the tree ready for Paul to open tomorrow morning.'

'You're amazing! Thanks. Any man would be lucky to have you. Just remember that.'

'You're biased, but thank you. I'll try… I'll text soon to update you.'

I ended the call, put my dressing gown on and went into the living room to get my coat, which was resting on the arm of the sofa. I reached into the pocket to get the toy.

It wasn't there. Shit.

Don't panic. It's fine. It'll be here. Somewhere. It had to be. I checked the other pocket, then turned them both inside out before looking on the floor and down the side of the sofa. Still nothing.

But I'd definitely had it after we'd finished ice-skating. I remembered pushing it down so it wouldn't fall out. I even remembered it being there when I got my coat from the cloakroom after we'd been to the bar. So where was it?

Fuck.

My stomach sank as I realised the place it was most likely to be. Back at the hotel room. It must have fallen out.

Why, God, why?

That meant I'd have to go back.

It was just approaching one o'clock, so if Nicolas was cutting Yvette's hair at two, he wouldn't have checked out yet. It should still be there. That was at least a relief.

Although going back was the last thing I wanted to do, I had no choice.

I flung on some clothes, quickly threw my hair up in a ponytail and pulled on my coat, then put on my boots. I thought back to what that bitch had said about them. How did she know my 'Uggs' were fake? Did rich people have some sort of radar to pick up on these things? I couldn't justify paying so much for the real ones, and they were comfortable. I'd had them for years, so it was true they'd seen better days, but when I'd got dressed to go out yesterday, I hadn't known I was going to end up staying in one of the fanciest hotels in London, being judged by a stuck-up cow.

Anyway, I didn't have time to tart myself up. I had one goal: finding that toy for Paul. I didn't care if Yvette or Nicolas thought I looked like a downtrodden pauper. They'd just have to accept me as I was. I had zero fucks to give.

Just because Christmas had been ruined for me, there was no way I was going to let it be a disappointment for Paul. Tomorrow needed to be perfect for him, and if I had to come face-to-face with Nicolas to help make it happen, then that was exactly what I was going to do.

CHAPTER FIFTEEN

B y the time I arrived at the hotel, I was filled with DGAF gusto.

It was like a light bulb had gone off in my head. I was annoyed at myself for allowing things to get to me for so many years. Angry for how I let my boss treat me. Paying me peanuts when I deserved a lot more. I was good at what I did. But because I'd allowed him to make me feel small, I'd stayed there, thinking I wasn't worthy of finding another job and I wouldn't find somewhere better.

I was also frustrated at myself for not walking away from my relationship with Jasper sooner. Or speaking up about how his family made me feel.

And I was pissed at letting that Yvette cow talk to me like that. Like I was some worthless gold digger. Less than something she found on the bottom of her shoe. Although I'd assumed at the time that she was Nicolas's wife and I was worried about being some sort of homewrecker, I still should have stood my ground and said my piece.

But no more. I didn't care if she was the Queen of

Sheba or if Nicolas was French royalty or something, I wasn't going to let them make me feel inferior anymore. It was time to make changes, and even though the New Year was still a week away. I wasn't going to wait until then to make a resolution. The changes had to start right now.

I stepped out of Green Park station and took out my phone. Once I'd realised I'd lost the toy, I'd told Bella I needed to go back and she'd said to text her once I'd arrived at the hotel and found it. She still felt bad about me coming all the way to hers, so she was going to see if she could meet me somewhere closer once Mike and Paul were back with the car or send a cab to collect it.

Just as I started walking towards the hotel, I felt something solid in front of me.

Shit. I'd done it again. Bumped into someone whilst I was on my phone. I really had to get out of that habit.

'I'm so sorry.' I pressed send on the message, locked my phone, then pushed it into my pocket.

'We have to stop meeting like this...'

I looked up. My eyes almost popped out of my head.

It was Nicolas...

'Oh... I...' My stomach flipped. I didn't even know what to say. I wasn't expecting to meet him here. I was ready to storm up to his room and show him and that cow of a client that I wouldn't be a pushover anymore.

'I have been calling you. Please can we talk?'

I was about to say no, but then I remembered why I was here. I had to get the toy.

'Okay, but on one condition... there's one thing I need from you.'

'Tell me.'

'I think I left something in your room, so I need to come up and find it.'

'Was it this?' Nicolas pulled the dancing milkshake from his pocket.

'Thank God!' I jumped on the spot with relief. 'Yes! That's it! Thank you!'

'I saw it on the floor where you had dropped your coat and I thought it could be important. That was one of the other reasons I was calling you. I want to tell you that I had found it, but you did not answer your phone.'

'I'm sorry, I just...' God. So much for being more assertive.

I paused. My mind raced. I needed to collect my thoughts. Fast.

The way I saw it, I had two choices: thank Nicolas for returning the toy and for an amazing day yesterday, put it down to experience and walk away, or be brave, tell him that I really liked him and see if there was any way that he liked me back. And when I say *like me*, I meant enough to be more than just a Christmas fling. The chances of him wanting that were slim, but I hadn't liked anyone this much since... well, forever. Even in the early days of dating Jasper I didn't remember feeling like this. So maybe I should try. Nothing ventured, nothing gained.

'Let's walk.' I gestured towards Green Park. 'Look. I haven't done this whole one-night stand stuff before. Seeing Yvette, your client, this morning threw me. She made me feel like shit. And when I found out you were loaded, it just brought back the memories of my ex and I freaked out. The truth is, I like you. I know I shouldn't because this was just a bit of fun to you and you live in another country, but I do.'

There. I'd said it.

Strangely, as difficult as it was to be honest and lay my heart on the line, I was glad I had. I didn't know how or why I felt so drawn to Nicolas, but I did and Bella was right. It wasn't easy to find a connection with someone. So if I told him how I felt and he didn't feel the same, I'd know that I tried. At least that way, I couldn't have any regrets.

'Cassie—*ma chérie*—I like you too. That was what I was trying to tell you. I feel this could be something special. I want to explore it. Take it further. When I woke up this morning, I felt *fantastique*. The best I had felt in years. It was not just sex, which of course was beautiful, it was *you*. You did something to me. That is why I want to spend the day with you. I hoped that we would have breakfast, a walk before lunch, then after I do Yvette's hair, we would be together, for my last few hours here.'

'Oh…' My stomach sank. That would have been amazing.

'I know we live in different countries, but Paris is just two hours on the Eurostar. It is not very far, *non*? I would like to try to make this work between us. I do not want to say goodbye to you.'

My heart fluttered. He was serious. This was more than a fling to him. It didn't have to be over after all.

'I'd really love to try too.' I smiled. 'But I don't want to get hurt. I still have reservations about the whole money thing. I'm tired of people making me feel like I'm not good enough and I don't want to get sucked into a toxic world again.'

Nicolas stopped and took my face in his hands. 'I hope that I have never made you feel that way.'

Now that we were talking calmly and I thought about it, he hadn't. He'd been nothing but a gentleman. I was wrong. He wasn't like the others.

'You are more than good enough for me,' he continued. 'I know you have doubts, but I promise to try my best to prove that *I* am good enough for *you*. To have someone like you in my life would make *me* the lucky one.'

Hearing those words made me melt faster than a snowman under a blowtorch. That was so sweet. And I could tell by looking in his eyes that he was genuine. He was speaking from the heart.

'That means a lot,' I added.

'Please do not worry about the money. It is all still new to me.'

That was interesting. I didn't realize he'd only recently become rich.

'What exactly do you do? Are you some sort of French hairdressing celebrity who styles kings, queens and snooty rich bitches like Yvette?' I laughed. I hadn't bothered to ask him earlier because I'd assumed we wouldn't be seeing each other again, so there was no point.

'Not exactly. I was a hairdresser. I still am, but only for special clients.'

I raised my eyebrow.

'When I say *special*, I do not mean...'

'It's okay, I was joking.'

'Oh! So yes, just for some clients. Now I own a hair tools company called Icon...'

'*You* own *Icon*?'

'*Oui.*'

'So *that's* how you were able to get the hairdryer so easily!'

'Well, yes. If I had my phone, it would have been easier. I could call my office. But then my team would want to talk about emails, messages, sales, meetings and…'

'And you came to London to switch off from all that.'

'*Exactement.*'

'So how come Andrew had a hairdryer?'

'I work with Andrew yesterday morning. He cut hair sometimes for the homeless, which is something I like to do in Paris, and he ask if I can help. A few days ago I send some tools for him to use in the salon to say thank you for invite me. So I promise to send another dryer if he give that one to you.'

'Wait, what? You cut hair for the homeless?'

'*Oui.* Not as often as I want. Just when I can. People pay a lot of money for me to do their hair in the salon and now they pay a lot for my products. So it is just a small way to help people without good fortune. Of course, if you are on the street, you worry more about if you will have food or somewhere to sleep, so a haircut is not a priority. Most people say no at first, but when they say yes, it can help them feel better. Even for a few moments.'

My heart was so full it could burst. Here was someone who was obviously minted, but he didn't just sit in his ivory tower barking orders at his minions and counting his riches. Instead he tried to give back. I wished there were more people like Nicolas.

'Wow. That's incredible.'

'*Merci.*'

'And I *love* your brand. Everyone says you make the best straightening irons, curling tongs and hairdryers. I'm not just stroking your ego. They're literally what every

woman on the planet—well, the ones I know anyway—
want to find under the tree. I even asked for the irons for
Christmas when I saw Santa yesterday.'

'Really?' His eyes widened. 'I can arrange that.'

'Oh no.' I winced. 'I wasn't fishing for freebies. I just
think it's so cool you own that company.' Now that I
thought about it, that was probably why he'd said the
receptionist at Andrew's salon couldn't take payments. I
bet Nicolas wanted to give me the dryer for free too.

'It has not been easy. It took many years to create the
products. I had to find money to pay to research, develop,
design and advertise them… so many costs. I had very
little sleep because I have to work in the salon in the day
then work on the products at night. But when they launch,
they become successful quickly. Not just because the products deliver well, but also because my clients are very
supportive.'

'I can imagine if you've got rich and famous
customers, that really helped spread the word. They're
obviously very influential. Your products are literally
everywhere.'

I always saw his tools on the pages of glossy maga-
zines and in the salon, and celebrities and influencers were
constantly raving about them on Instagram.

'*Merci beaucoup*. I still have a lot of work to do. That
is the thing. I want my business to be a success, of course.
But I am always busy working, which is not good. It is
important to enjoy life. Have time to relax. The last few
years have been very intense.'

'I bet.'

'I do not complain when I say this. It has given me a
nice life. More than I could imagine. Travel first class, stay

in nice hotel, eat at glamorous restaurants. Sounds perfect, *non*? But it can be lonely. And what you said earlier is true. Sometimes it still feels like another world. That is why I did not tell you everything when we met. For one night I want to feel normal again. Relax. Do normal things. And turn off from everything.'

'Is that why you didn't bring your phone?'

'*Oui*. When you call me phone robot, it was true. I have it with me always. For once, I want to remember how it feels to not answer calls and emails. I just want to walk around London. Feel free. Live in the moment. Experience simple things that people enjoy at Christmas. Do you understand?'

'Absolutely.'

Relief washed across Nicolas's face. I hadn't realised when I'd accused him of being a phone zombie that I'd struck a nerve. It must be hard to go from having a normal life to running a hugely successful business really quickly. I didn't blame him for wanting to have a break from it all.

'I am very happy to hear you say that.' Nicolas took my hands in his.

'And I can see now why you didn't want a relationship either. You must be so busy.'

'I have bad experiences with women recently. My ex did not want to work. She just like to spend my money and go to fancy parties.'

Ah. So that was what he'd meant when he'd made a comment about women being superficial and only being interested in men with money.

Nicolas explained that the last thing he wanted was to meet another money-hungry woman. When we'd met, like me, he'd just wanted some time to breathe and be alone for

Christmas. No women and, apart from that one client, no work.

'That is why I know you are special, Cassie. You did not know about my money and you still like me.'

'Well, I definitely didn't when we first met!'

'*C'est vrai*. You think I am dickhead.'

'Exactly! But now I think you're okay.'

'Just *okay*?' Nicolas wrapped his arms around my waist and pulled me in for a long, slow kiss.

'Maybe you're a little bit more than just *okay*.' I grinned.

'I am supposed to attend a grand Christmas lunch tomorrow in Paris, but now all I want is to stay in London a little longer and relax here with you. What do you think? Would you like to spend Christmas with me? For us to be together?'

'Are you joking?' My eyes widened and my heart sprung to life again. 'I'd love that!' I threw my arms around him. Spending Christmas Day with Nicolas would be the best. 'Would we stay at your hotel?'

Maybe people would think I was crazy, but as appealing as it might sound to spend Christmas Day at a posh hotel, I kind of wanted to chill at home. It wasn't a big deal if we had to. I was sure enjoying several courses of top-notch food served in luxurious surroundings wouldn't be a hardship. The location wasn't important, though. Being with Nicolas was what mattered.

'If you want, but I was hoping we could spend it at your place?' said Nicolas. He'd read my mind. I knew I liked this guy. 'If that is okay with you? It would be good to have Christmas in a real home. Sit beside a Christmas tree. Watch movies on the sofa…'

'That sounds perfect! The only thing is, I don't actually have a tree…'

'Oh yes, I forgot. You do not like Christmas.' He rolled his eyes.

'Well, I *didn't*. But then I met somebody who changed my mind…'

'Really?' He smirked. 'I am *very* happy to hear that…'

Before I could catch my breath, Nicolas pressed his lips on mine and gave me the sweetest kiss. God. I could snog this man forever.

Nicolas pulled away slowly.

'What is the time?' He rolled up his sleeve to look at his watch. 'That is good. We still have time to find a tree and take it to your place.'

'Seriously?'

'*Bien sûr*. Christmas is not Christmas without a tree.'

'But what about Yvette?'

'She has gone. One of the advantages of money is that I do not work with clients I do not like. I have concerns about her before, but when I discover that she almost make me lose the best thing that has happened to me in many years, that was something I could not forgive.'

'Wow… thanks.' I paused. 'That is if it's me you're talking about?'

'Oh… this is embarrassing. Actually, I was talking about somebody else…'

I folded my arms.

'*Je plaisante*. I make a joke. You *know* I am talking about you.' He stroked my cheek.

'Thank God for that!' I chuckled. 'Okay, *monsieur*. I'm definitely up for buying a tree, but we have to get this toy to my godson first.'

'*Pas de problème*—is not a problem.'

The idea of spending more time with Nicolas filled me with excitement. And we were getting a tree! It felt like ages since I'd had one at home. Maybe we could get some decorations and crackers too? This was a special occasion, so we might as well go all out. I couldn't wait.

Looked like Christmas was back on after all.

CHAPTER SIXTEEN

I t was Christmas morning and I felt amazing. Just like I
had yesterday.

After we'd made up in the park, I'd called Bella to
arrange getting my gift to Paul. In the end, we'd decided
putting it in an Uber would be the quickest and easiest
option. Nicolas had offered to pay, but I'd said I had it
covered. Just because I'd discovered he was loaded didn't
mean I was going to start milking it.

When I'd checked the price, it wasn't too bad. The fare
would be less than a couple of drinks in a London bar, and
Paul's happiness was worth more than that.

Bella had texted to confirm it had been delivered safely
and was wrapped and ready to place under the tree once
Paul was asleep. She promised to send a video of him
opening his gift too. I couldn't wait to see his little face.

Nicolas and I had found a tree and bought loads of
decorations. We just about fitted everything in the people
carrier he'd booked to take us home.

We spent hours decorating it. Mainly because we

rewarded ourselves with a glass of French wine Nicolas had chosen at the supermarket. It was *so* good. I always felt so overwhelmed with all of the different choices, but he knew exactly what to pick. Oh, and we might have also been distracted by kissing under the mistletoe we'd got several times too. One thing might have also led to another, resulting in a very enjoyable Christmas Eve *session* on the sofa.

Mmmm...

I got the tingles just thinking about it.

Anyway, when we eventually finished, the tree looked amazing. We'd opted for red and gold baubles, festive ornaments, frosted pinecones, sweeping gold ribbons instead of tinsel and twinkling fairy lights. We couldn't find any stars, so got an oversized red bow to put at the top. It looked so pretty.

Nicolas carried me to bed around midnight and now here I was. Well rested and waking up on Christmas Day with a hot French guy beside me.

Thank you, Santa.

I went to the kitchen to get a glass of water. It was only eight in the morning. I washed up the dishes from last night and tidied up the kitchen. Once Nicolas was awake, I'd ask him what he wanted for breakfast and we could enjoy it in bed with a glass of Bucks Fizz. What a way to start the day.

Just as I was heading back to the bedroom, I saw Nicolas in the living room.

'Oh my God!' I laughed.

Nicolas was lying naked on the sofa with the giant oversized bow strategically placed below his waist. It just about covered his modesty. He looked delicious.

'I am your gift.' He smiled.

'I love it!' I climbed on top of him and gave him a long kiss.

'Did you look out of the window?' Nicolas asked when we came up for air.

'No? Why?' I went and opened my blue living room curtains.

'No way! Oh my God!' The ground was covered in the brightest, whitest snow. It looked so pretty on the rooftops and dusted on the branches of the tree across the road. 'It never snows on Christmas day!'

'I told you that this Christmas would be different. That it would be better for you.'

He did. And look: it was Christmas morning and I wasn't sat on the toilet suffering the after-effects of food poisoning and I hadn't been dumped or involved in any cringeworthy incidents (that Yvette woman yesterday didn't count).

Now that I thought about it, as awful as those bad events had felt at the time, some of them had happened for a reason. The guys that dumped me weren't right for me anyway. If I'd stayed with that jackass Jasper, I wouldn't be with Nicolas now. Bella was right. The universe (and maybe even Santa) had worked their magic.

'So what do you say?' Nicolas stroked my face. 'You would like to unwrap me today and *encore* in the future?'

'Yes, please!'

Although it was obviously very early days and trying to make a long-distance relationship work was going to be a challenge, for once I was optimistic about my love life.

I still had a lot more to learn about Nicolas (or Nico, as I now liked to call him, which he said he preferred to

Queue Jumper and *dickhead*). But already I could tell he was different from the other guys I'd met. And he wasn't like the rich people I'd encountered either. Not all men were arseholes and not everyone with money was snooty or treated me like I was inferior.

Yep. I reckoned Nico and I could really have a future together. I could feel it in my gut.

'*Bien*. Now I can give you your second gift…'

'You got me another gift?'

'Of course. It is Christmas! Check your message.' He tapped away on his phone.

A WhatsApp notification sounded. I picked up my phone, which was still on the coffee table where I'd left it last night. There were two missed calls from Spencer. I couldn't believe he'd called me at ten o'clock in the evening on Christmas Eve and at seven thirty this morning. On Christmas Day. Well, actually I could. I wouldn't be responding and I definitely would be handing in my notice in the New Year. I'd get another job.

Spencer had always made me feel like I was inferior and didn't have the skills to find a new position, but he was wrong. I might not have done well academically, but at this stage in my career, that shouldn't even matter. I was dedicated, thorough, and organised and had a lot of experience behind me, so I'd be fine. It was time for a fresh start.

I ignored Spencer's voicemail and opened Nicolas's message.

'What?' I screamed. 'Wow! A ticket to Paris!'

'You have shown me around your beautiful city and I want to do the same for you. What do you say?'

'I say *oui, oui, oui*!'

'I like it when you say that.' He kissed me slowly.

'Now let me see if I can do something else to make you say *oui*, over and over again...'

Even though the day was still young, as Nicolas took me in his arms, I knew that this was going to be the best Christmas *ever*.

Up until forty-eight hours ago, I'd always associated Christmas with bad things. But now that I thought about it, I had a lot to be thankful for. I had family and friends who loved me, food in the fridge, a roof over my head and good health, which was a lot more than many people. And to top it all off, I had a kind, funny, mega hot Frenchman by my side. Things on the romantic front were finally looking up.

Right now I was feeling grateful. My fortunes *had* changed. And something told me this was the beginning of a new and exciting life.

Yep. Turned out, I really *was* lucky after all.

Want more?
Would you like to know what else Cassie and Nico get up to on Christmas Day? Join the Olivia Spring VIP Club and receive the *My Lucky Night* **Bonus Chapters** for **FREE!** **Start reading now:** https://BookHip.com/HNWJJQM

Book 3 Is Coming!
Want to find out what happens when Cassie jets off to Paris to see Nico? Will she fit in with his millionaire lifestyle or feel like a fish out of water? **Pre-order *My Paris Romance* from Amazon now!**

ENJOYED THIS BOOK? YOU CAN MAKE A BIG DIFFERENCE.

If you've enjoyed *My Lucky Night*, **I'd be so very grateful if you could spare two minutes to leave a review on Amazon, Goodreads and BookBub**. It doesn't have to be long (unless you'd like it to be!). Every review – even if it's just a sentence – would make a *huge* difference.

By leaving an honest review, you'll be helping to bring my books to the attention of other readers and hearing your thoughts will make them more likely to give my novels a try. As a result, it will help me to build my career, which means I'll get to write more books!

Thank you SO much. As well as making a big difference, you've also just made my day!

Olivia x

ALL BOOKS BY OLIVIA SPRING: AVAILABLE ON AMAZON

The Middle-Aged Virgin Series
The Middle-Aged Virgin
The Middle-Aged Virgin in Italy

Only When it's Love Series
Only When it's Love
When's the Wedding?

My Ten-Year Crush Series
My Ten-Year Crush
My Lucky Night
My Paris Romance

Other Books
Losing My Inhibitions
Love Offline

Box Set
Ready To Mingle Collection

The Middle-Aged Virgin

Have you read my debut novel ***The Middle-Aged Virgin***? It includes Bella from *My Lucky Night* too! Here's what it's about:

Newly Single And Seeking Spine-Tingles…

Sophia seems to have it all: a high-flying job running London's coolest beauty PR agency, a long-term boyfriend and a dressing room filled with designer shoes. But money can't buy everything…

When tragedy strikes, Sophia realises she's actually an unhappy workaholic in a relationship that's about as exciting as a bikini wax. And as for her sex life, it's been so long since Sophia's had any action, her bestie has started calling her a *Middle-Aged Virgin*.

Determined to get a life and *get lucky*, Sophia hatches a plan to work less and live more. She ends her relationship and jets off on a cooking holiday in Tuscany, where she meets mysterious chef Lorenzo. Tall, dark and very handsome, this Italian stallion might be just what Sophia needs to spice things up in the bedroom…

But the dating scene has changed since Sophia was last single, and although she'd score an A+ for her career, when it comes to men, she's completely out of her comfort zone. How will Sophia, a self-confessed control freak, handle the unpredictable world of dating? And how much will she sacrifice for love?

Join Sophia today on her laugh-out-loud adventures as she searches for happiness, enjoys passion between the sheets and experiences OMG moments along the way!

Here's what readers are saying about it:

"I couldn't put the book down. It's **one of the best romantic comedies I've read**." Amazon reader

"Life-affirming and empowering." Chicklit Club

"Perfect holiday read." Saira Khan, TV presenter & newspaper columnist

"Olivia has an innate knack for the sex scenes, which are very hot. **This book was steamy**, but with such a huge element of humour in it that when you read it **you will certainly giggle throughout at the escapades**." Book Mad Jo

"Absolutely hilarious! A diverse, wise and poignant novel." The Writing Garnet

Buy *The Middle-Aged Virgin* on Amazon today!

AN EXTRACT FROM THE MIDDLE-AGED VIRGIN

Prologue

'It's over.'

I did it.

I said it.

Fuck.

I'd rehearsed those two words approximately ten million times in my head—whilst I was in the shower, in front of the mirror, on my way to and from work…probably even in my sleep. But saying them out loud was far more difficult than I'd imagined.

'What the fuck, Sophia?' snapped Rich, nostrils flaring. 'What do you mean, it's over?'

As I stared into his hazel eyes, I started to ask myself the same question.

How could I be ending the fifteen-year relationship with the guy I'd always considered to be the one?

I felt the beads of sweat forming on my powdered forehead and warm, salty tears trickling down my rouged cheeks, which now felt like they were on fire. This was serious. This was actually happening.

Shit. I said I'd be strong.

'Earth to Sophia!' screamed Rich, stomping his feet.

I snapped out of my thoughts. Now would probably be a good time to start explaining myself. Not least because the veins currently throbbing on Rich's forehead appeared to indicate that he was on the verge of spontaneous combustion. Easier said than done, though, as with every second that passed, I realised the enormity of what I was doing.

The man standing in front of me wasn't just a guy that came in pretty packaging. Rich was kind, intelligent, successful, financially secure, and faithful. He was a great listener and had been there for me through thick and thin. Qualities that, after numerous failed Tinder dates, my single friends had repeatedly vented, appeared to be rare in men these days.

Most women would have given their right and probably their left arm too for a man like him. So why the hell was I suddenly about to throw it all away?

Want to find out what happens next? Buy *The Middle-Aged Virgin* on Amazon today!

Love Offline

Have you read my fourth novel *Love Offline?* Here's what it's about:

Looking For Romance In Real Life…

Emily's Struggling To Find Romance Online. Will Ditching The Dating Apps Lead To True Love?

Online dating isn't working for introvert Emily. Although she's comfortable swiping right in her PJs, the idea of meeting a guy in person fills her with dread.

So when her best friend challenges her to ditch the apps, attend a load of awkward singles' events and find love in real life, Emily wants to run for the hills.

Then she meets Josh. He's handsome, kind and funny, but Emily's had her heart crushed before and knows he's hiding something…

Is Josh too good to be true? Can Emily learn to trust again? And if she does, will it lead to love or more heartache?

Love Offline is a fun, sexy, entertaining story about friendship, stepping outside of your comfort zone and falling in love the old-fashioned way.

Here's what readers are saying about it:

"This book spoke to me on soooo many levels!! I loved the realness this book shows!!!! Five stars." **Once Upon A Book Review**.

"The perfect mix of a sexy, hot, modern day romance, wit and just an all out bloody fabulous book! Highly recommend. Five stars." **Nicole's Book Corner.**

"Fun, flirty and fabulous... I was laughing throughout the whole book. Five stars." **Reading In Lipstick.**

"Hilarious, sexy-romp with heart! I adored the relationship Emily has with her best friend Chloe." **A Girl With Her Head Stuck In A Book.**

"If you are a fan of Sophie Kinsella and Lindsey Kelk, then this book is for you! *Love Offline* is a romcom for the modern woman." **Girl Well Read**.

"This book just makes you feel good and all fuzzy inside, def one to curl up with on the sofa with a cup of tea. Five stars." **Barbs Book Club.**

"I loved the refreshing take on love and dating in this book....Definitely recommend!" **Nic Reads In Heels**

"A sexy little chick lit read...A lovely, modern story involving friendship and falling in love." **Mrs L J Gibbs**

"I loved Olivia's last book, but I think this one was even better. Five Stars" **Hayley Jayne Reads.**

"Pure Perfection. Five stars." **Head In A Book 18**

Buy *Love Offline* on Amazon today!

AN EXTRACT FROM LOVE OFFLINE

Chapter 1

Normally, I love social media.

The endless fancy food and envy-inducing holiday pics on Insta, the witty conversations on Twitter, the funny memes on Facebook—I adore it.

When I've got important designs to create for clients and deadlines to meet, I can often be found spending many minutes (truth be told, more like hours) scrolling through strangers' feeds rather than *actually* working. After all, who doesn't like staring at photos of cute kittens?

Like I said. Normally, I *love* social media.

Well, I *did* until precisely 9.29 a.m. today.

The day started off like any other Monday morning. Hitting the snooze button a dozen times before finally crawling out of bed. Having a shower whilst wondering why the weekend flashes by in what seems like five minutes, whereas Monday to Friday lasts for half a century. Throwing on whatever looked clean and didn't need ironing, then dragging myself to my local coffee shop to get the caffeine-and-sugar hit I needed to help me feel remotely human, or at least alert enough to start work.

I'd sat at my desk, taken a generous bite of my blueberry muffin, sipped on my steaming latte and switched on my computer. I had considered going through my emails but, in true procrastination style, decided to check Instagram first instead, because of course that was *much* more important than doing actual work.

And there it was.

That photo.

The picture, which had already amassed thirty-six likes.

The image that instantly made my head spin and my stomach sink.

Captioned with just three words that sent my world crashing down.

She said yes!

My ex-boyfriend Eric, who I always believed would be the man I'd spend the rest of my life with, had proposed to Nicole—the woman he'd been cheating with for the last six months of our relationship—and she'd said yes.

Great.

There they were on what looked like some tropical beach, waves crashing against the golden sand, gazing into each other's eyes, lips locked, her left hand strategically placed on his shoulder, showing off the giant rock adorning her ring finger.

Exactly what I *didn't* need to see on a miserable grey March Monday morning in South London.

After staring at my screen for longer than was healthy, I'd tried to do what any smart, sensible, level-headed, pragmatic woman would if she heard the news that her unfaithful ex was marrying the younger model she'd been traded in for. I'd told myself I couldn't care less, that it was his loss, there were plenty more fish in the sea, karma would catch up with them and to just get on with my day.

Did it work?

Of course it bloody didn't.

So instead I'd dragged myself the ten steps from my home study to my bedroom, put on the 'Life Sucks' Spotify playlist, curled up into a ball and sobbed until my mobile rang.

It was Chloe. She'd heard the news from a friend during the school run and was on her way over. *With cake.*

I'd told her I wasn't sure that even a Victoria sponge the size of the Atlantic Ocean could make me feel better, but she'd insisted. And now she had let herself into my flat using the key I'd given her for emergencies. I suspected that she was probably mentally preparing herself for the sight that was about to greet her.

Chloe knew how much I loved Eric and how I'd struggled to get over him, so she'd realise that this wasn't going to be pretty.

'Emily Robinson!' she shouted, bursting through the bedroom door. 'Up you get!'

I slowly peeled my head from the pillow and tried to gauge whether I really had to force myself off the bed and deal with the situation or if I could get away with lying here for the rest of the afternoon and convince Chloe to give me a bucketload of tea and sympathy.

Who am I kidding? This was my no-nonsense best friend. And she did *not* do self-pity. Especially over an unfaithful man.

'Come on, Em. We're not doing this again. Remember?' She picked up my iPad from the bedside table, frowning as she bashed away haphazardly at the screen before eventually managing to pause the playlist. 'No more listening to sad songs. No more tears over Eric. He's not worth it,' she said, edging closer to the bed. 'You can do *much* better than that tallywag.'

I slowly dragged myself upright, scraped my thick, dark curly hair off my face and tucked my knees under my chin.

'I know he's a loser, but seeing that picture, of *him*, with *her*, proposing after knowing her for all of two minutes, when he *knew* I'd wanted to get married for *years* and constantly fobbed me off, it just—it really hurt,' I said, using the sleeve of my grey jumper to wipe the tears streaming down my cheeks.

'I understand that,' said Chloe as she smoothed down the back of her 1950s-style polka dot dress and sat down on the plain magnolia duvet. 'But you really need to move on, Em. It's been seven months. It's time to start a new life. Unfollow the fool like I told you to ages ago and make new friends.'

'I make new friends all the time,' I scoffed. 'I'm up to almost six hundred on Facebook. Admittedly, Insta is lagging behind a little as I'm low on content, but—'

'For crying out loud!' Chloe crossed her arms. 'I don't mean friends on social media. That's nonsense. I'm talking about *proper* friends. You know, people that you speak to face-to-face in a restaurant, rather than clicking the stupid love heart button on a post of some person from Timbuktu that you've never met.'

Trust Chloe not to understand. She's so old-fashioned, she doesn't even own a smartphone. Can you imagine?

'I know you have an aversion to technology and anything online, Chloe, but social media has been my lifeline. If you think I'm bad now, I would have been *much* worse without the support of my online community.'

'Your *online community*?' Chloe rolled her eyes. 'Good grief! Sounds like some sort of cult!'

'Laugh all you want, but their likes, comments and uplifting posts have kept me going.'

'*If you say so,*' replied Chloe, reaching in her bag and pulling out two forks, serviettes and a container before taking out a large slice of chocolate cake. The rich scent filled the room. *Mmmm*. It smelt delicious. 'Like I've said before, I really think you should venture out of these four walls and try new things. You work from home all day, and apart from coming round to mine, you never seem to go anywhere. If you had a load of hobbies and were out making new friends in real life, you wouldn't have time to think about what that idiot is doing. You'd be too busy having fun.'

Here we go again. It's the *you need to get out of the flat more* lecture. I love Chloe, I really do, but she just doesn't get it.

My whole social circle revolved around my life with Eric. His friends became my friends, and after the breakup, that disappeared overnight. Now it was almost impossible to find anyone to go out with. On the rare occasions that I *did* get invited out, all the people in the group were coupled up and I was the odd one out. I got treated like either a weirdo or a potential husband thief. That's when I wasn't getting pitied or being shown photos of other random single men they were convinced would be ideal for me, purely because we'd both been 'condemned' to a life of solitude. I shuddered just thinking about it. *No, thanks*. I'd rather sit at home and have conversations online than be subjected to that hell.

'It's not that simple,' I huffed as I reached for my own slab of sponge and took a large bite. I wasn't in the mood to use a fork and serviette like Chloe. 'Everyone I know is married and has kids and doesn't have time to go out.'

'I appreciate what you're saying,' said Chloe, stroking her raven bob, which she'd styled into her signature vintage waves. 'But you are not the only thirty-five-year-old singleton in London. There are *loads* of other people out there just like you, so if your old circle of friends doesn't fit your life anymore, make a new circle. Find new friends. Look.' She stood up. 'I hate to leave you like this, but I've been called into work today, so I've got to run. I'll call you later, but please—don't sit here moping. Go for a walk to clear your head and have a think about what I said. There's a whole world out there. So many exciting things you could be doing with your life, but you need to actually step outside of this flat to discover them. Promise you'll give it some thought?'

I looked up at her, fighting the temptation to roll my eyes after hearing her make the same suggestion for the millionth time.

'Yes, yes,' I said. 'I'll think about it.'

'And you'll stop thinking about Eric too?'

'Yes,' I muttered reluctantly. What was I supposed to say? It wasn't like I *wanted* to think about him. Eric was just always there. Right in the front of my thoughts.

'Excellent!' She smiled. 'You'll feel *so* much better

when you do. You don't need his toxic energy around you. Anyway, I'd better go.' She leant forward and hugged me tightly before rushing towards the door. 'Make sure you get stuck into the cake. Love you!'

I stretched over to the container and grabbed another helping of sponge, shamelessly stuffing it into my mouth, then wiped my fingers before wrapping the duvet tightly around me. Getting out of these four walls? Going for a walk? *Not a chance.* That was the last thing I felt like doing. I planned to stay right here in this flat until I ran out of food or was forced to evacuate due to a state of national emergency. Whatever happened first.

Want to find out what happens next? Buy *Love Offline* on Amazon today!

ACKNOWLEDGEMENTS

Can't believe this is book number eight! This novella would have been much harder to write without the support of the following wonderful people.

Firstly, I'd like to thank my lovely mother. I really appreciate your advice, guidance and speedy reading of my early drafts.

Second shout-out goes to the amazing Emma – otherwise known as the queen of Christmas books! Thank you sooo much for your incredible enthusiasm and for providing such fantastic feedback. You've been flying the flag for my books since the beginning and I really appreciate all that you do.

Big thanks to my fantastic editor, Eliza, proofreader, Lily, cover designer, Rachel, and website designer, Dawn. Your expertise always gives my books extra sparkle!

To my darling: thanks for your unwavering support. Releasing two books in two months has been challenging, but you helped to make it so much easier.

Thank you Loz, Brad and Jo as always for reading early manuscripts and providing feedback.

A million thank-yous to the brilliant book bloggers who read, review and shout about my novels. Your support really makes a huge difference.

And the biggest, most heartfelt thank-you goes to *you,* dear reader. Thank you for buying, reading and recommending my books. It's because of you that I'm always excited to get to my desk and create more stories.

Until next time!

Olivia x

ABOUT THE AUTHOR

Olivia Spring lives in London, England. When she's not making regular trips to Spain and Italy to indulge in paella, pasta, pizza and gelato, she can be found at her desk, writing new sexy romantic comedies.

If you'd like to say hi, email olivia@oliviaspring.com or connect on social media.

facebook.com/ospringauthor

twitter.com/ospringauthor

instagram.com/ospringauthor